MIND

vs.

MATTER

KONRAD KOENIGSMANN

outskirts
press

Outskirts Press, Inc.
http://www.outskirtspress.com

ISBN: 978-1-4787-6598-1

Outskirts Press and the "OP" logo are trademarks belonging to Outskirts Press, Inc.

PRINTED IN THE UNITED STATES OF AMERICA

*This book is dedicated to my parents
for their unceasing support
and for inspiring me to
keep on going with this book.*

TABLE OF CONTENTS

Prologue

A SHOCKING EVENT

"And please welcome our CEO, Marcus Delaney, to the stage at our Fifteenth Annual Product Showcasing of Cybor Technology." Marcus Delaney walked onto the stage in front of an expectant audience of thirty-five thousand. He was a small man with balding hair, and he looked to be around sixty. He wore an immaculate bone-white tuxedo, with a pin-striped purple and yellow tie and a pen in his shirt pocket. The audience roared and gave him a standing ovation as he came on. "Welcome, welcome to you all," he said as the audience gradually quieted. "It has been fifteen years since I founded this humble, little company (at this, some people laughed), and today I believe we have truly created the best product we have ever made. (He said this every year and then presented the best product of the year.) I call it the Eye Spy 0.2.

"To let someone give only a vague explanation of the Eye Spy 0.2 would undermine the value of the product, so now please welcome my chief scientist, Kaspar Gurov."

As soon as Marcus Delaney stopped speaking, a thin, tall

Russian man walked onto the stage. He looked to be around forty, with jet-black hair. He received a smattering of applause from the audience. "Welcome to all of you," he began with a slight Russian accent. "As Marcus Delaney told you, I chief scientist to him, and I now explain newest invention I made for him.

"Eye Spy 0.2 is going to be pioneering technology in field of implants. It is essentially camera implanted in one eye, which contains supercomputer also. With camera in eye, you can take picture of whatever you see, without inconveniences of real camera. You can zoom, pan, and so on. It will be the camera that can take anything the eye can see. Now you see, but how to control this camera? This is where supercomputer comes into equation. Supercomputer in implant will connect to brain through optic nerve, so camera controlled by thought. With supercomputer also comes bonus of having increased intelligence, and you become a living, organic computer in essence. Everything that you can do with real computer can be done with supercomputer. When we tested this camera in mice, they became very intelligent, as intelligent as average human. Think what this means for our intelligence. This can lift our civilization to new heights. In fact, we have just started our first human trials. I, Kaspar Gurov, am the first test subject. On the screen above me, you will see what the camera implanted in my eye sees. I will then give series of commands that correspond with my thoughts for a demonstration of the technology."

The lights dimmed and the low humming of the projector became audible. On the screen, an image of the audience came into view, with various digits and symbols scrolling across the sides of the screen. The audience oohed and aahed with expectancy. Gurov cleared his throat. "Computer, provide my general information and vitals," he enunciated clearly. Instantly, the screen changed into lines of scrolling green text that read as follows:

> Name: Gurov, Kaspar. Nationality: Russian. Age: 42. Born: October 23, 2003. Family: Gurova, Nataliya, wife; Gurov, Vladimir, son. Occupation: chief scientist, Cybor Technology, Inc. Achievements: PhD in molecular biology from the University of Oxford, winner of the Nobel Prize in biology (the first person to do so), inventor (supposedly) of 435 objects, including Eye Spy 0.2. Heart rate: 83 bpm. Blood pressure: 90/70 (normal). Weight: 202 pounds. Eye color: hazel. Hair color: black. Estimated life expectancy (based on various factors): 56 more years.

As the text finished scrolling, the screen returned to its former view of the audience. "Take a picture of the person sitting in the forty-third seat of the sixty-second row and show it to me," commanded Gurov. The camera panned to the sixty-second row, then zoomed in on the forty-third seat, and took a picture of the bewildered old man in the seat there. More text scrolled:

> Completed objective: take picture of person in forty-third seat of sixty-second row.

As soon as it was confirmed that the old man sitting in that seat had been correctly identified by the computer as the person sitting in the forty-third seat of the sixty-second row, the audience applauded heartily.

"Identify all members of Cybor Technology sitting in the audience, and then state their names and occupations at Cybor Technology," continued Gurov. The computer identified Cybor Technology employees, their status in the company, and where they were sitting. The camera then took a picture of each of them. The audience applauded louder and louder with each successful identification. When the identification process finally ended, Kaspar Gurov cleared his throat again. "Identify any employees from rival companies, and show the same information as for Cybor Technology employees." Again the computer successfully completed the task provided. The audience dissolved into a mass of appreciative roars. Marcus Delaney had truly been right this year, thought some. This really was big.

In his makeshift office offstage, Marcus Delaney smiled as he watched the proceedings. His smile grew even bigger when the offers to buy tens of millions of Eye Spy 0.2s began to flow in like a river bursting a dam. Some people were going to have their personal fortunes grow exponentially in size.

Outside, the audience quieted down again as the computer finished. Kaspar Gurov did not know it, but his next command would be the last thing he would ever say. Some people would get the money that Marcus Delaney was making, just not anyone from Cybor. Gurov opened his mouth and prepared to speak. "Identify any threats to me or anyone else affiliated with Cybor, and send people to eliminate them," he commanded. A deathly silence fell over the audience as everybody realized what Gurov had just said. Text scrolled on the screen:

> Sixty-seven threats identified, elimination of
> targets commenced.

In the sudden silence that filled the room, a slight pinging sound could be heard. Kaspar Gurov slowly fell backward, clutching at a spot on his neck, and hit the stage with a heavy thump. Blood dripped out of his neck onto the floor. He was dead.

At almost the same moment, six gunmen stormed into Marcus Delaney's office. The expression on his face changed from anger to surprise to fear in an instant. "Greetings from *Meister* Liebnitz," said the leading gunman with a smile. He raised his pistol and shot Delaney through the head three times. He was dead before hitting the floor.

All around the world at the same moment, armed gunmen stormed into the offices of the Cybor board members and shot them. The gunmen were all in the employ of one shadowy figure: Karl von Liebnitz. Known throughout the world by different aliases, he was considered a terrorist by almost every country and one of the most dangerous men in the world. However, he had made sure that he would not publicly be known as the mastermind behind the Cybor attacks for a long, long time. The self-styled successor of Osama bin Laden, Liebnitz's ultimate goal was to unify all the countries of the world and then become the monarch of that new country, thus gaining control of the entire world. He wanted to go further than any terrorist had ever gone and go down in history for the ages.

In the seconds after Kaspar Gurov died, the crackling sounds of gunfire could be heard outside, along with a lower, more sinister-sounding boom. With a crash, the doors to the hall were blown away, revealing the battle going on beyond them. Heavily armed gunmen were fighting the security guards, and they were overpowering them through sheer numbers. Just as the doors were blown apart, the gunmen dispatched the last of the guards. The hidden sniper who had killed Gurov dropped onto the stage from the tangle of rafters above, and the rest of the gunmen swarmed through the doors and sealed off the exits. Everybody tried to rush the exits, but the first ones to get there were callously gunned down. Then the man who had dropped onto the stage spoke. "Stop moving," he said in a cold, commanding tone with a slight German accent. Not everyone obeyed him though, and a few more gunshots rang out. "If you do not stop moving, everyone in this room will die. If you stop moving, you have a slight chance of living on as prisoners."

The statement made the rest of the audience stop moving and the gunmen lowered their weapons. "*Gut* that we are all quiet now, *ja?* You may be wondering whom my men and I work for and who the man is that wants to take over Cybor Technology from Marcus Delaney and his associates. You have most likely heard the name of my Meister before. His name is Karl, Karl von Liebnitz." As the sound of his voice subsided, the entire audience erupted with gasps. After the gunman's statement had sunk in, he continued, "I am one of his most trustworthy military commanders, Yuri Klatschnikov. You see, my great Meister wants to take over the world, and the takeover of Cybor Technology, well, that is a very important step in the great master plan." Everyone in the audience knew of Karl von Liebnitz's great plan. Certainly, everybody must have watched when Liebnitz hacked the networks and spread the messages, and everyone here preferred to call him by his infamous nickname: the Red Widower. But no one in the audience knew why Cybor Technology was so important to his plans.

"I assume from the bewildered expressions I see that you do not understand why Cybor Technology is so important to my Meister's master plan. Well, I will tell you why." Klatschnikov proceeded to explain why Cybor Technology was so important to the master plan. His explanation evoked a surprising amount of whispering and drawn-in breath from the audience. Klatschnikov smiled.

It was not a smile one would enjoy seeing. His smile contorted his face into a leering mask of evil. The effect was multiplied by the fact that he had an ugly scar running down the side of his face, and it only became fully visible when he smiled. Klatschnikov waited for the audience to become still again. "Why would I tell you what I have just explained to you? Because my Meister ordered it, and *nein*, he is not stupid. All of you knowing about it is of no consequence because it will probably be the last truthful thing you will ever be told, and you will most likely be my Meister's prisoners for the rest of your lives. Initially we would only have overrun Cybor Technology at the end of our Meister's conquest. However, at that time Kaspar Gurov had not yet 'invented' the Eye Spy 0.2. That product will still be marketed as it would have been before this coup; it will just be under our Meister's direct control using our new puppets on the board. I cannot tell you why the Eye Spy 0.2 is important to us or anything else. Now that I have finished telling you everything that must be said, I can leave with my gunmen. You will be locked in this hall until my men come back to pick you up." Klatschnikov turned to leave but stopped to make a parting remark. "Oh, and one final piece of truthful advice: never trust a rogue...or a terrorist. *Tschüs, Freunde.*"

With those final words, Yuri Klatschnikov took his gunmen and left. What people in the audience would never know is what killed them...or when it killed them, for Yuri Klatschnikov had actually given them a good piece of advice: never trust a rogue or a terrorist. He had lied to them about being taken prisoner. Klatschnikov had been ordered to set bombs throughout the building. Karl von Liebnitz did not work with loose ends. Prisoners could escape, no matter how careful he was, and escape to tell everyone what he had planned, and having that information released prematurely would be calamitous for him.

As soon as Klatschnikov and his men were out of range of the bombs, Klatschnikov took a transmitter out of his pocket and pressed its big red button. Behind him, a cloud of smoke and flames rose up, along with the humongous roar of an extremely powerful explosion. There was no sound of shattering glass or cars thrown through the air. Anything and everything touched by the blast was instantly incinerated without a sound, leaving behind only ash.

His task complete, Klatschnikov took an encrypted phone out of his pocket. It had only one number. He pressed a button and made the call. The voice on the other end of the line was garbled by a voice scrambler. "Ja?" said the voice. "Meister, *hier spricht Yuri*," replied Klatschnikov. "Objective has been completed." The voice on the other end replied, "Is this true,

Yuri? You have completed the objective? Gut, gut. Look for potential replacements for the board whom we can manipulate with ease. Come back to base for your reward, Yuri." The line clicked and Klatschnikov hung up. He stood there and smiled and then began to laugh. His laughter dissolved into a mass of cackling and screeching as he thought of his reward.

Halfway across the world in a small village near Budapest, Hungary, a man huddled behind a trash can, wet and soaked to the bone from the freezing rain that mercilessly fell that day. He was hiding behind the trash can more for show than anything else, since he highly doubted that the killers would find him now, not after he had hidden himself away so well. Apparently, God cared for him on this day, for at the moment, only he knew that he was alive. This man's name was Will Hartford.

Will was around thirty and had been on the board of Cybor Technology. He had survived the murder attempt through a premonition. Had God given him that premonition? But why would God do that? To him, God was nothing more than a useful entity in the sky who sometimes greased the wheels of action and helped Will continue on his merry path to the top. His body double had gone to the office that day instead of him. Yes, Will was paranoid enough about being murdered that he kept a body double for just that purpose, no matter what kind of death had been planned for him. He had fled to this miserable little dump of a village only because he kept money here in case of an emergency like the current one. In his eyes, sitting behind a trash can was a necessary evil so he could wait for the inhabitants of the village to go to sleep before retrieving his money.

He was a believer in God in the days when no one believed in God anymore because God was a useful tool to have when one had great ambitions. Will had curly blond hair and blue eyes. He was one of those men so rare nowadays: completely and utterly honest on the outside, yet having the machinery of a ruthless man on the inside, one who would stop at nothing to get what he wanted. Ironically, he hated lies and felt a simmering hatred when forced to listen to lies told to him. Yet his entire life was based on a web of lies. He considered himself exempt from his lofty ideals. In Will's eyes, he was one step above the ranks of most men.

He was not from rich origins. He earned his fortune after Marcus Delaney had hired him fresh out of graduate school. Delaney had quickly recognized his ruthless abilities and killer mind-set for what they were, and Will had risen quickly through the ranks to become a member of the board, the youngest and newest member. He did not know who had attempted to murder him, but he could assume it was the leader of the gunmen swarming out of the building that contained his office. He could also assume that the gunmen were employed by someone who gave them their singular-looking uniforms with shifting camouflage and hidden weapon packs. Their employer must have targeted the rest of the board as well so he or she could take over Cybor Technology. There was only one man who could fulfill every single requirement, when the requirements were combined with prior knowledge: Karl von Liebnitz.

For months the board had had numerous tip-offs from

various spies that ever since Kaspar Gurov had "invented" the Eye Spy 0.2, which Liebnitz had found out about through his network of hidden spies, Liebnitz had moved Cybor to the top of his priority list of targets to capture. Thus, attacks on the company were imminent. No one had taken the threat as seriously as Will, and he had predicted that the attacks would come on the day of the exhibition, where the technology and Delaney would be exposed. Will took every death threat very seriously as his death would spell a huge loss to the world community in its current corrupt condition. Liebnitz would obviously leave no loose ends, so Will had prepared for months to flee on the day of the exhibition. He feared he had been right and assumed that Delaney and the rest of the board were dead. Not that most of those doddering fools were much of a loss, but they were better than what Liebnitz would replace them with.

Will knew that he had to go into hiding, but he did not know whom he could trust to not betray him to Karl von Liebnitz. He knew that by now his most trusted servants would already be dead, and he was officially on his own. First, though, he needed to procure a disguise so he could safely go and buy supplies for himself. He would definitely be identified without a disguise, being a famous figure on television, he assumed. If people knew he wasn't dead, Liebnitz would find out, and there would be men looking for him for whatever exorbitant reason Liebnitz could think of.

In a secret underground bunker in a secure location, Karl von Liebnitz felt satisfied. The first step of his master plan had been initiated. Now he had the Eye Spy 0.2 in his hand. The product would obviously go on the market and bring in more money than his other operations could give him, but he would have to get his scientists a sample of the implant and have them immediately begin work on an improved version of it for his soldiers. He most definitely saw flaws in the current version, and those would have to be ironed out. Were they the normal Gurov-type errors? If so, his scientists would probably have to redesign the entire product to make it remotely useful. He would see what the news had to say about his latest antics. Of course, he might be suspected, but that suspicion would not last long. There were, after all, no witnesses, and his puppets, when put in place, would snuff out any rumors.

Liebnitz congratulated himself on a good day of work and went to sleep a happy man before continuing his operations the next day.

The only thing that would have soured his day would have been if he had known that a board member, especially that Hartford snake, was still alive. But of course Liebnitz knew nothing of that, and so Will Hartford was able to live on in peace for a long time. His disguise was so effective that he even got married and had a son. He named him Pierre. Perhaps he was daring God to make his son great by naming him in the French style after Peter, that great disciple of Jesus. In fact, Will got God to bless his son with a great destiny and an unspoken prophecy. Pierre would grow up and do great things, but that would be twenty-two years in the future when the great chain of events would begin. They were in fact activated by Pierre himself and had much to do with his father, Cybor Technology, and Karl von Liebnitz.

1

A NARROW ESCAPE

Twenty-two years later, 2067

It was 6:30 a.m. The alarm started beeping. I groaned, hit the snooze button, and tried to go back to sleep. College and its stupid rules about when to get up. Can't they let a guy catch some decent sleep? When I complained about this, they told me to go to bed earlier to get more sleep. But they knew full well that they gave us too much homework to be able to go to bed early. The only time I ever like getting up is when I'm having one of those dreams.

It's always the same dream. A man is walking away with masked men while a building is blowing up behind them. For some reason I always feel a surge of panic and terror when I look at the man's face, and I want to wake up, but I can't. Then the man has a horrible, twisted smile. He says, "Where is your father, boy?" I'm paralyzed, and then an alarm wakes me up.

The good thing about college: it's nowhere near as strict as my dad.

I've always thought Dad has been a bit strange. Not nuts, but strange. It's not that he isn't kind to me or that I feel abandoned by him; it's just that there's something…off about him and his actions, something that I can't quite place my finger on. I've never stayed in one place long enough to make lasting friends. Every few months, Dad moves to another place. Dad is the only person I have. I've never known Mom. Sometimes I wonder who she could have been. I wonder if I'll ever find out. Dad never mentions her or anything related to her. The most conceivable reason I can think of is love that should never have been. They got married but realized they could never be a family after I was born, so they mutually agreed to part ways, and I got left with Dad.

Sometimes, I'm envious of other guys at college when I see their mothers visiting them. They've had something that I'll never have, something they should cherish and never regret. They might not always want a mother, but they would understand how it feels to not have a mother if they were in my position. Sometimes Dad can be loving and caring, and sometimes he can be irrationally unreasonable and paranoid to the point that it becomes an obsession. That's where a mom would step in.

I don't know anything about Dad's past, but the way we move every few months and how sometimes he looks around nervously as if someone's following him makes me suspicious of something beneath all the glitz and glamour. He's so careful and vigilant and doesn't let me form long-lasting relationships with friends. They're always such shallow relationships.

I think Dad is running away from the past that's trying to come back and haunt him. Most people are OK with seeing and confronting their past, but not Dad. There are two possible reasons Dad would be afraid of the past: either he was a criminal and was wanted somewhere by someone, or he was an important person many years ago and had to go into hiding because someone wanted him dead.

There is one incident that always comes to mind when I think of the second possibility: the Cybor incident. It happened twenty-two years ago. Supposedly, the entire board was murdered in a single night, and a new board was "elected." Everyone basically knew the worst-kept secret of the new board: they were puppets of Karl von Liebnitz, the famed Red Widower. That meant that Liebnitz was gaining access to the lives of the billions of people who had bought one of the Eye Spy products. But why would he take twenty-two years to consolidate his power while virtually disappearing off the face of the earth? Everyone knew his plan to take over the world and realized this takeover was the first step of a world coup.

If Dad had been a board member, someone wanting him dead would be a justifiable reason to keep on running. But even if someone thought that one was dead, running helped prevent discovery to the contrary. I truly hope that Dad had been a board member. That would explain everything Dad has done over the years he's been my father. Unfortunately, I don't think Dad would tell me anything unless it's under extraordinary circumstances, but it isn't as if I'm hoping for my theory to be true. One of my most fervent dreams is to fight alongside Dad, to invent something with him. However, that will only happen if I know the truth that I think he's hiding: that he had been a board member. But I never reveal myself this way, my hopes, dreams, or thoughts. I've said too much. Pretend I never said anything at all.

Let's backtrack to the moment that I woke up. So the alarm was ringing. I groaned and groped around on the clock for the snooze button so I could get a few more minutes of sleep. Then it hit me as it does every morning: there is no snooze button on these stupid college alarm clocks. You can't even turn them off. They can only be turned off from within the system. They even sense if you aren't getting up and become more annoying. Reluctantly, I rolled out of bed and went to put on my clothes. The dining hall would close promptly at seven o'clock, so if I wanted any chance of getting the good dining hall food, I had to run to get it now; otherwise, I would have really bad food or none at all, and that really sucked, especially when lunch was only served at two o'clock. Oh man, I'm getting too far ahead of myself today. I even forgot to tell you what college I attend: MIT, the Massachusetts Institute of Technology.

When I got to the dining hall, I realized that I shouldn't have run after all. There was some sort of holdup, and the line extended back for three blocks. Jeez. I asked the guy in front of me, "Excuse me, do you know what's going on here?" The guy answered, "Nope. I know as little as you do. I wonder what stupid thing it is this time. Last time it was because the president threw up on the breakfast counter." I laughed a bit. Delays like this happened all the time for such stupid and non-essential reasons that they sometimes made me wonder why everyone who went to MIT seemed to like this place.

Suddenly a murmur spread through the crowd. I wondered what was going on. Then I saw a familiar head of slicked-back blond hair snaking through the crowd. The president? What? Somebody must have been in a load of trouble. Why else would the president be coming? Suddenly the president stood before me. His face was grim. "Pierre Hartford," he said, "come with me. Now." His chilling voice cut through me like a knife. Was I in trouble? My heart sank like a stone. How? I couldn't be in trouble. When had I ever done anything that would get me in trouble?

Word spread through the crowd. I heard their shocked whispers. "Pierre? What?" "Never. Pierre's the best student here." "That can't be. Are you sure?" The president led me through the crowd. "We're going to my office," he said. "I have something very serious to discuss with you, Pierre. No, you're not in trouble," he added reassuringly. "It's about your father."

If my heart could have leaped and sunk at the same time at that moment, it would have. It fell because I sensed that Dad was in danger, and it leaped because maybe, just maybe, the moment of truth had come, and my dreams would be fulfilled...or crushed. I didn't want to think about the latter option. "My father, sir? What's wrong with him?" I replied. "I'll tell you everything in my office, Pierre. There's a person there that I'd like you to meet as well. He may help you realize what is going on," replied the president. Who would want to meet me that could help me and my dad? I pondered this question as the president and I walked to his office.

The president opened the door and beckoned me in. He looked around anxiously with the same vigilance as my father. So something *was* definitely wrong. "I instituted that holdup at the dining hall so I could search for you in the line, Pierre," said the president, whose voice began to crack. "Pierre, I believe that you and your father are in grave danger." The president locked the door behind me. "That is why I would like you to meet Christian Roland, the head of the Federal Bureau of Intelligence, or as you would know it, the new FBI." There was a man waiting for the president and me in the office. He didn't look special at all. I guess that meant he had already succeeded at half of his job if he was so inconspicuous. If I had passed him on the street, I wouldn't have thought that he was special at all. He looked to be around seventy, with gray hair. His face was lined with wrinkles, and he had a scar running from his right eyebrow to his left cheekbone. He wore a creased Yankees T-shirt that looked as if it were from the 1990s and jeans that were so old they were worn to the point that they had lost their color.

"Hello, Pierre," he said in a deep, gravelly tone. "I've heard quite a bit about you from your father. Your father and I are acquaintances." So it was the FBI that Dad had been using this time as a safety net. "You know my father, sir?" I replied. "Yes. I know your father because he was a board member of Cybor Technology," continued Christian Roland. My heart leaped through the ceiling. I was ecstatic that my hopes had been fulfilled. But then my heart sank at the prospect of the news to come. "Your father had supposedly been murdered in the attacks on Cybor twenty-two years ago, but we knew better after he had contacted us and moved to Cape Cod. We've discreetly been watching you and your father for years to prevent you from being murdered by the Red Widower, or Karl von Liebnitz. Not that your father needed much help on that front, as his constant vigilance and movement from state to state pretty much erased any leads that could have been found. However, we had our own reasons to keep your father under surveillance."

I could almost hear the unspoken words coming out of Roland's mouth: "You see, Pierre, sometimes your father, well, he can lose control, and we're trying to prevent that from happening." It was true that Dad had done some pretty impossible things, which I had witnessed, not that I got any answers if I asked questions about them. So the FBI had some freedom from the corrupt mass of red tape that was our government, since the FBI could actually think straight. I guess the relationship had to be pretty tenuous then.

"We also tried to prevent you from being put in the news," continued Roland, "but obviously Liebnitz found out about you due to circumstances we cannot control. The MIT newspaper published an article about you being the top science student and printed your last name, Hartford, which Liebnitz recognized. Violating principal freedoms by prohibiting that article from being run in the newspaper, well, you know MIT is an independent entity, and this would not have gone down well with the opposition parties, so our powers were pretty limited in that respect. We'll already be taking a lot of flak for extracting you from here."

Wait, what? An extraction? How'd the FBI even get a permit for extraction within hours? It usually takes years for an extraction request to be processed, and by then it's often too late. The FBI must have pulled out some serious stops. "So Liebnitz issued a death threat against you and your father. We deemed it necessary to step in with a more direct intervention to protect both of you," said Roland.

I started wondering if there was something special about me. Mr. Roland must have thought that I was discrediting his arguments with my thoughtful expression because he continued, "I know that this will be very disorienting to you, but it's true, Pierre. Doesn't this clear up so many questions you've had? Constant moves, always enough money even with the most ridiculous costs, how your father worked you, little things you've noticed, your father's disappearances, and so on. The list goes on and on. Don't these questions get answered by what I am telling you? Don't your wildest dreams get fulfilled?"

I started thinking. Everything Mr. Roland said was right. His statement explained everything. I had never known the source of Dad's money. When I was younger, strange men had visited him. They must have been from the FBI. But they gradually disappeared. Perhaps as the relationship dissolved, they pulled out more and more. That's why Dad always knew someone wherever we went. And our pattern of moving wasn't necessarily random. When we moved, I noticed that we seemed to be moving in an intricate pattern.

I wasn't quite convinced though that every word that Mr. Roland said was true. I needed concrete proof that Dad had really been a board member. After all, Mr. Roland was still not telling me everything. Perhaps this was his power play to wrest me away from Dad and toward the FBI because of my high potential as a spy, shattering my relationship with Dad and giving the FBI somebody to have more control over.

Mr. Roland must have seen my doubtful expression and realized what my doubts were about. He said, "You want concrete proof that your father had been a board member. Well, you should also know how you could even have been born. Your father's headquarters as a board member were located in Belgium—to be exact, Brussels. So what I am asking you now is a key to completing your puzzle. You know what *der Tag* is, right?" Now I was really confused. "*Der* what?" I responded. "Der Tag," replied Mr. Roland, "is German for 'the day.' " I thought for a second. "You mean the Cybor coup?" I asked. "Yes," replied Mr. Roland, "that's what I mean. Your father was supposedly killed. Haven't you seen the old newsclips? A building burned down in Brussels? A certain Will Hartford dead?"

I thought back. Now that Mr. Roland mentioned it, I had seen that Brussels clip. I had asked Dad, "Why does the dead man have the same name as you, Dad?" He had been very evasive then. "A coincidence," he had replied. That curt answer was all I had gotten from him. I had noticed, though, that strangely there was no picture of this Will Hartford. Mr. Roland began to have a glimmer of a smile as he saw my dawning recognition. "You have seen that clip," he said. "That Hartford was your father's body double. There was no picture because your father had it removed. This is your concrete proof. Do you believe me now, Pierre? If you don't, I have a special piece of proof for you: your first toy was a robot that you dubbed 'Thin Stick.' " Wait a minute. Dad wouldn't have just offhandedly given out that piece of information. That must mean that the relationship had been very close and that Mr. Roland had not shifted as far away from Dad as his subordinates had.

If I hadn't been convinced before, the last piece of information served to convince me. Only Dad and I could have known that fact, or anyone he had told that to, i.e., Mr. Roland.

Each explanation fit beautifully into my conundrum and completed the puzzle. "I truly believe you, sir," I said. "What do you still have to tell me?" Mr. Roland replied, "I'll tell you everything soon, Pierre, but first I have to get you out of here and to a secure location. Liebnitz has already dispatched men to capture you. We have to leave now." As if the moment had been planned, an alarm started to beep. "He's penetrated the perimeter," Mr. Roland muttered.

This was not the time or place to ask the questions I wanted to ask then. They would have to wait. I could tell that Mr. Roland was similar to Dad in this respect: he wouldn't take no for an answer, and his desire for self-preservation was extremely high during situations of high tension.

He rolled up his sleeves, revealing that his right arm was covered with devices. He spoke into one of them. "Bradley, Stevens, come back to the rendezvous." Through the transmitter a "Yes sir" was audible. Mr. Roland turned back to me. "Pierre, put your hand on my watch," he said. "Why, sir?" I asked. "Just do it, Pierre," he snapped, visibly losing his composure. By testing the waters, my hypothesis had been proven correct. No wonder Mr. Roland and Dad had been close. I timidly obeyed and put my hand on his watch. It began to beep.

Suddenly there was a knock at the door. The president hurried over and unlocked the door. Two burly men rushed in. "They're coming, sir," said one of them. Mr. Roland pressed a button on his watch. "Activate the defenses, Stevens," he said. "And then get ready to leave." One of the men pulled a metal cube out of his pocket and typed in a code on the surface. The cube unfolded into a large device, almost the size of a small computer. Then he handed it to the president, who took it, though with some reluctance.

"Mr. Downs," said Mr. Roland, "you know what to do. The defenses should buy you enough time for a full evacuation. Good luck." The president nodded. I felt full of dread. All this just because of me? I must be a very important pawn in the chess game of eternity. Mr. Roland pressed another button on his watch. "Get ready, Pierre," he said. His watch began to beep rapidly. Suddenly I was enveloped in purple light. I began to spin slowly in circles. Faster and faster I spun. Then I was absorbed by the light. The room dissolved into nothingness, and I was gone, along with Mr. Roland.

I opened my eyes to find myself no longer spinning but moving through a void with Mr. Roland. I must have closed my eyes when the room dissolved. I looked around. Nothing seemed out of the ordinary for a void. These structures had been discovered and observed before. Just pure energy buzzing around that could theoretically be tapped into, white streaks of light against a murky background. Then I looked at Mr. Roland.

I was shocked by what I saw. Mr. Roland looked to be thirty and in his prime. But just minutes ago, he had been around seventy. Even as I watched, Mr. Roland seemed to be aging backward into a gangly teenager. Soon he had become a squealing baby. I said, "Sir, what is happening to you?" Or at least I said those words in my head. No sound came out of my mouth. It was as if my lips were glued together. I tried again.

With an immense effort, I repeated my sentence and heard it come out of my lips in proper English, not gibberish. So the void was better left alone and undisturbed if it took a great effort to even speak. A fragile balance was keeping the void from collapsing, but that must mean that we were in a wormhole. So the FBI must have developed a miniaturized superparticle accelerator inside the watch to rip space-time.

Mr. Roland, who had been aging back again, abruptly opened his eyes. He looked straight at me. His face bore an expression of shock. That must mean that usually forces were too strong for normal humans to speak in the void, so I was special in some way. I wanted to say more, but suddenly there was another flash of light and I began spinning.

When the spinning stopped, I let go of Mr. Roland's watch. I saw that we were in a dark metal room. Was this a secret FBI base that I had been taken to? Where else could I have been taken? Next to me, another flash of light signified that the agents had arrived as well. I felt disheveled, and the agents looked disheveled. So everybody had aged, which meant we had traveled backward in time to the apex and forward to our destination.

Mr. Roland composed his facial features before turning to face me. "What your father said is very, very true about you, Pierre. Perhaps he did tempt some force of nature. Well, you'll talk to him in a minute. I'm taking you to see him."

2

A WIDENING CHASM

Mr. Roland led me down a dank, dark hallway. "What is this place?" I asked. "It's a decommissioned NSA [National Security Agency] base," he replied. "When the FBI took over operations from the NSA and renamed itself, we decided that this was a good place for a secret base, hidden from Liebnitz. You're safe here, Pierre." As safe as I possibly could be, I thought. "Where are we, exactly?" I asked. "We're in the Mojave Desert," replied Mr. Roland.

"So sir," I said. "How exactly did we get transported here?" Mr. Roland smiled. "You're a smart boy. Try to figure it out."

My mind began reflecting on the dilemma. If Mr. Roland had gone through the aging process, we must have traveled through the fourth dimension, which meant that it was indeed a wormhole. "You're telling me," I began with disbelief, "that the FBI has managed to create a wormhole generator for teleportation usage by miniaturizing a superparticle accelerator into a generator the size of a watch?"

Mr. Roland began to clap louder and louder while smiling. "Your father said you were smart, but not that smart," he exclaimed. "My God, you are right. But how we discovered the technology is a conversation for another time. We've reached our destination."

Mr. Roland stopped in front of a nondescript door. He typed in a code, and a scanner began to hum. "Pierre," he said, "put your finger on the scanner, please." I did as he asked. The gel that had been placed over the scanner was soft and squishy. When the device had scanned me into the system, Mr. Roland put his own finger on the scanner. The door slid open noiselessly. "Go on," said Mr. Roland. "I'll be waiting right outside here."

I took a deep breath and stepped in. The room was a mass of blinking control panels and beeping detectors, with banks of computers stacked against one wall. "Pierre," said a voice in the shadows, "welcome to the new headquarters of the Liebnitz Counteroffensive." Dad stepped out from behind a computer he had been fiddling with. He was sweating and looked haggard.

"Dad," I said, "it's good to see you." He ran over and hugged me tightly. "I know that you have a lot of questions," he said, "but please hold them until I tell you my whole story. Sit down. This is going to take a while."

I eased myself into a chair. It was surprisingly comfortable. "I was born in Leipzig, Germany, to poor Greek immigrants," he began. "That was in the year 2015. Although my parents did not have much, they had enough to give me a proper education in a decent school. I learned to speak German and English fluently. I also changed my name from its Greek form to English.

"During my childhood, a boy lived down the street from me. He was about five years younger and a true German. He was a queer boy and never liked to talk much, but when he did talk, his words rang through the air with importance. His name was Karl von Liebnitz. One day I managed to make his acquaintance. We became fast friends. We were both very sharp, you know, and very bright for our age. When we participated in national contests together, we would alternately finish first and second. As a team, we were unstoppable. Our bond was strong and enduring, or so I thought.

"However, I didn't like that Liebnitz was so arrogant and abused his intellect at times. He hacked into the foreign ministry's website once for fun. This created some friction between us but not enough to break off our friendship. The real break came when I was eighteen and Liebnitz was thirteen. We had applied for the only opening at MIT that year, along with thousands of others. We knew that one of us would get in and that one of us wouldn't. Liebnitz was passionate about this opening and very focused on getting in. However, in the end, I was accepted. He was not.

"He grew angry with me, saying I had sabotaged his application so he would be denied acceptance to MIT. He called me a cheat and a liar and denounced me as a friend. Oh, if I had just kept my mouth shut, but I retorted in turn. We grew so incensed at each other that Liebnitz hurt me quite badly. Our friendship was shattered and thrown into the fire after that. I still saw him around in the neighborhood before setting off for the United States, but we ignored each other. I saw that he had a band of lackeys trailing him. Liebnitz must have convinced them through brute force. Among his band were

Yuri Klatschnikov, David Bartleby, and Ramon Joubert; those lackeys formed his original organization. If I had known what he was doing, I would have stopped him. But I had no idea and thus set off for MIT.

"At MIT, I discovered something very strange about myself. Whenever I used mechanical parts to assemble any object, I had a natural, intuitive way that was more efficient than the official instructions. When I was alone and pondering a solution to assembling an object, the pieces assembled themselves like magnets! I was astounded. Was this some sort of secret power I possessed? I noticed more things. I began to invent things, thought in more technological terms, and became more creative in general. I marveled at the changes coming over me. If I had been a genius before, what was I becoming now?

"My PhD advisor suggested that I seek a coveted job opening at the premier technology company of the time: Cybor Technology. I applied and was accepted. I was a regular employee until Marcus Delaney met with me one day alone and saw my great skill with assembly and invention. He was so impressed that he gave me a large raise and a promotion. I became his rising star. Within three years of joining the company, I joined the board."

Dad paused. "Are you saying, Dad, that it was you who turned Karl von Liebnitz into a terrorist?" I asked incredulously. "I'm not proud of what I did that day," responded Dad, a note of bitterness creeping into his tone. "But the past is the past, and if he felt that way, then he deserved my berating. Continuing on," he said, preventing a debate on the morality of his actions. Dad was hiding some things, I could tell, but I decided not to press the issue.

"So I was on the board. I need to explain to you the global situation from when I was born until 2043, when I became a board member. In 2015, we still had 193 countries, although Ukraine soon fell into Russian hands and Syria was conquered by the Islamic State, which in turn was conquered by Saudi Arabia, among other happenings. But you already know this world history. Russia and the United States warred over Ukraine; the US clashed with IS over Syria; India and Pakistan got into spats; terrorist cells grew out of control everywhere; and Europe managed to implode inward. Thus, World War III was a free-for-all. Despite utter chaos, the United Nations stayed strong and kept the nuclear codes hidden. This was a big contributor to the swift ending of the war. Eventually, after years of useless combat and needless bloodshed, a treaty was signed and land partitioned, much to the disapproval of the UN. The United States got North America; Brazil got South America; the United Kingdom and Germany divided Western Europe; Russia took Eastern Europe; Egypt and South Africa divided Africa; Saudi Arabia took the Middle East; China took the rest of Asia; and Belgium and Hungary formed an alliance, retaining their independence. And so began the second Empire Age. After that debacle, the UN lost all credibility and became little more than a puppet, much like the predecessor, the League of Nations. I became a dual American and German citizen and set up office in neutral Belgium.

"Now let me explain to you the systems of Cybor and the events leading up to today from the time I became a board member. As soon as I became a board member and set up office, I was contacted by the FBI, which had already merged with the NSA by then. The FBI wanted me as a spy in Cybor.

As a matter of fact, so did the German spy agency. I became a de facto double agent, but my first loyalty was to the United States. Liebnitz had emerged with his organization, which was called *Tyrannei*, and the peace became strained as the balance of power tipped. Tyrannei attracted poor immigrants from all over Germany. They were promised food and training. Liebnitz was inspired to destroy the world and reform it in his own way. His first disciples didn't need much urging, seeing who they were.

"When Liebnitz developed his sophisticated spy network, he sent some spies to Cybor. As part of the FBI, I was helping to rebuild the FBI's own networks and new bases to be resilient against Liebnitz, knowing his strategy best as a childhood friend. I retooled the Cybor business after finally convincing the board to immediately shut down the weapons division and focus on developing cyber-defense products. As a spy, I shuttled information from the German spies to the FBI. Knowing Liebnitz's tactics of hiding in the most obvious disguises, I managed to catch one of his spies: Kaspar Gurov.

"An imperfect Russian at best and a complete mess at worst, Gurov was a total failure at everything and a perfect spy per Liebnitz's standards. Who would think that a dreamy bumbler could ever be a competent spy? However, his clumsiness cost him, and I caught him one day. I threatened him with imprisonment, and so he became the FBI's direct conduit to Liebnitz. We fed him information; he gave us back more.

"I realized some very deep things during the Gurov years: outside of the FBI and Tyrannei, which were enemies tearing at each other, the world was inherently flawed and broken. I began to see that the world had to be reformed but in an un-Liebnitzian way. I realized the top of the pyramid was the rotten core of the apple. Just being on the board, I saw how petty, arrogant, and corrupt Marcus Delaney and his cronies were. I began to see the need for reform, not just on a person-by-person basis, but on a worldwide scale.

"I devised a plan to draw out Liebnitz by exposing Gurov. Gurov was chief scientist by virtue of some bribes fed to some of the less intelligent members of the board. I used his stupidity to my advantage and designed a flawed Eye Spy 0.2 prototype for him. I gave him the instructions, and he copied them to make a machine. I wrote the code, designed the parts, and made him the first test subject for the convention in Washington.

"As expected, Gurov told Liebnitz about the Eye Spy 0.2. Liebnitz ordered him to lie low for the attacks on the day of the convention, again as I had expected. Gurov informed the board. I had already prepared my body double for times when dangerous events could occur that might kill me, and I prepared him again. Liebnitz knew that the board had found out about and discounted the plans for the attacks. Gurov, blindly trusting the board, in his sheer stupidity decided to disobey Liebnitz.

"On the day of the convention, Liebnitz's men infiltrated the building with Klatschnikov at the helm to eliminate Gurov. He also set up men in the regions of the board members' offices. You know what happened on *der Tag*, Pierre. I have evidence because Klatschnikov left behind the casing of the bullet he shot into Gurov, and the FBI found it.

"By the time the attacks came, I was long gone. I had a chance to tell the other members to move, but they deserved their deaths, just as Gurov did and Liebnitz will. The world is corrupt, and they were at the core of the problem. The world must be cleansed of the disease before it can be rebuilt in an uncorrupt way.

"After I had fled from Brussels to Budapest, I escaped to Cape Cod with you, a tiny baby, to contact the FBI. I kept constantly moving, hiding from Liebnitz. But MIT was lax and published your name. Liebnitz connected the dots. And now we're here, son."

After my father had finished, I sat in shocked silence. "You let the board members die," I said hollowly after a while. "You let them die. It's not morally right to let humans die when you have the chance to save them, Dad." My father burst into anger. "The world is corrupt," he screamed. "It must be cleansed! A few deaths cannot stand in the way of a reformation to cleanse the world of disease!"

I was shocked, angry, and saddened. "First you expect me to follow you like an obedient little lamb and then give up my *morals*? What are you, crazy? Then you don't even talk about my mother and just gloss over her. I already know how bad your reply will sound to me, so I'll just leave now. I will see you then, *Father*," I said stiffly. I got up, wheeled around, and left. "Pierre," my father cried desperately. "Come back! Please! I still need to talk to you. Pierre...," my father said, his voice trailing off. Without looking back, I walked through the open door. Back inside, my father burst into tears.

I had gotten the truth at last, but I did not feel any better for it. The truth had stabbed me to my core, disturbing my moral values and creating a heavy weight in my chest that I had to live with.

3

THE BEGINNING OF THE OFFENSIVE, THE IMPOSSIBLE TASK

A third-person perspective: the fight for MIT

A university in Cambridge, Massachusetts, had prepared for war. War had arrived. The men of Karl von Liebnitz, commanded by Yuri Klatschnikov, had come for one and only one person: Pierre Hartford. Pierre Hartford was gone, but who were they to know that yet? The defenses were ready, and the evacuation of MIT had commenced.

Mr. Downs was standing, seemingly shell-shocked, and staring at the spot where Pierre and Mr. Roland had disappeared. He was brought back to his senses by his secretary bursting into his office. "Sir," panted the secretary, "set up the defenses. They're coming." Mr. Downs pressed a button on the metal cube he had received from one of Mr. Roland's men. Immediately, an energy field popped up around the campus, and an automated defense system was activated and revealed, covering all angles and routes into the university. Yuri Klatschnikov's advance scouts stopped in their tracks. Soon Klatschnikov arrived and stopped next to his scouts. He took his transmitter out of his pocket and called Liebnitz. "Ja?" said a garbled voice. "Meister," replied Klatschnikov, "as expected, the shield and defenses have been set up. Should I wait for the tanks and jets, or should I act now?" "Act now," replied the voice. "The longer you wait, the greater the chance that the Hartford boy is *weg*." Klatschnikov said, "Very well, Meister," and hung up.

Meanwhile, the students were loaded into carrier jets. Only Mr. Downs and his guards stayed behind. "The ships are ready to take off, sir," said the secretary through a videophone. "Take off in T-minus two minutes, or as soon as the defenses are breached," replied Mr. Downs. "Ten-four, sir," replied the secretary.

The defense system was quite special indeed. Commissioned four years ago, the system had been specially designed by the FBI to protect Pierre when he came to attend MIT. It included various advanced technologies: an electromagnetic disruptor shield that disabled most standard-issue weapons of the day and was also acting as a force field, laser stun guns, rocket launchers, ice beams, disassembling bullet sponges, and automatic ballistic missiles. This kind of a defense system was unprecedented among university campuses. Most had simple laser defense systems, easily obtained on the market.

Outside of a shield generator, Klatschnikov shrugged his shoulders slightly. Out of his shoulder pads, there came a sheet of armor that unfolded like origami and pulsed with electronic signals. Soon Klatschnikov was encased in a sheet of opaque black armor, with a black faceplate highlighted in neon orange. His forearms were covered in electronic dashboards, and his palms had faintly glowing rings on them. Klatschnikov raised his left hand. He was generating an electrostatic field in an embedded mini-generator. When his hand was fully charged up, he reached through the electromagnetic shield as if it weren't there and pressed his hand against one of the shield generators. Almost immediately, the defenses turned on Klatschnikov and fired projectiles, but they all shattered or bounced harmlessly off his armor. When his hand touched the generator, the entire shield crackled with an overload of energy. A bolt of lightning streaked from the top of the shield. After a few seconds, the shield along with the weaponry system failed as the weapons' cores overheated. But the cameras did not fail. They continued recording the events that happened next. Whoever watched the recording would be shocked. Klatschnikov had effortlessly disabled one of the premier defense systems in the country by deploying an electrostatic field and a set of shuritanium armor. Apparently, the weapons could not penetrate shuritanium, the strongest material ever discovered, possessing the unique property of being able to interface with any electronics attached to it and making any armor designed with shuritanium basically invincible.

Alarms began wailing inside MIT. Mr. Downs sent the order to launch the ships. Immediately, the stubby jets took off for Washington Air Base at Mach 7. Klatschnikov sensed that the Hartford boy was not on one of those jets. He would not have been sent off to Washington, where he would be tangled in a bureaucratic nightmare. Klatschnikov and his men rushed in, just as their fighter jets soared in and began to bomb the campus with their supersonic missiles. The tanks rolled in and fired frag shells. Klatschnikov ran swiftly through the halls, artfully avoiding the falling shrapnel, zeroing in on Mr. Downs's office.

Mr. Downs heard the alarm and began to quiver. He maintained his composure enough to initiate the self-destruct sequence of the cube. He knew that the valuable files were safe, and so was Pierre Hartford. He began counting the seconds until his death and the first blood of the war. Klatschnikov burst into the office. As soon as he saw Downs alone, he knew that the Hartford boy was gone. He howled in anger and shot Mr. Downs without a second thought. Blood spurted from Mr. Downs's neck, and he died, falling to the floor. Klatschnikov cursed bitterly. He withdrew the men from the university and let the tanks and jets blow MIT into oblivion.

Secret FBI base, the next morning

"Pierre," said a whispery voice through my mist of sleepiness. "Get up. Now. Quickly. Something has happened that I need to show you." I opened my eyes and saw Mr. Roland shaking me. I got up quickly and followed him. "What has happened, sir?" I asked. "It's better if you see it for yourself, Pierre," replied Mr. Roland. "This event can speak for itself."

Apparently, Mr. Roland had brought me to my room last night after I had collapsed into a crying heap, and the door had slammed shut behind me. At least both sides felt the same way. But it was a new day. I was refreshed and ready to roll. Mr. Roland led me back to the dreaded room. Father was there, waiting for our arrival.

"Will," said Mr. Roland, "show us the newest video." Father complied silently. I watched as MIT came into view on the projection. "They battled here, sir, after I had left with you, right?" I asked. "Yes, Pierre," replied Mr. Roland. "But just watch what happens now. I'll explain it to you afterward."

I watched intently. The campus seemed quite peaceful. Suddenly, however, a line of running gunmen came out of no-where. They stopped in their tracks when a shield generator came up. The camera was switched, and I could see the ad-vanced defense system in place. Wow. For MIT to have this type of a system was groundbreaking. And to keep this hidden from me while I was at MIT…wow. The camera switched back to the gunmen, and I could see a lightly armored figure stop in front of the shield.

He talked into his transmitter for a few minutes. When he put it away, he shrugged his shoulders slightly. A full set of opaque armor folded out of his shoulders. I could vaguely make out that his hands were covered in mini-generators. He raised his left hand, and it began to crackle and fizz. When he had built up enough energy, he moved forward. All sorts of projectiles were shot at the man, but they shattered or bounced off his armor! He walked through the shield as if it didn't ex-ist. He laid his hand on a shield generator. The entire shield fizzed, and a bolt of lightning shot out of the top of the shield.

When the fizzing died away, the shield was gone. The defense system was out of commission. Effortlessly, the gun-men swarmed MIT, but I could see that the evacuation of the students and valuable documents had finished. The jets had soared overhead and were long gone. Mr. Downs still stood in his office when the man in the armor burst in. He saw no one but Mr. Downs and seemed to howl. He shot Mr. Downs and left.

The gunmen withdrew from the campus. Tanks and jets had arrived. They bombarded the campus, and it blew up into a million pieces.

When the projection finished, I realized that tears were streaming down my face. Mr. Roland came over to comfort me. "It's OK, Pierre," he said. "When the war is over, the school will be rebuilt. Nothing of any significance has been lost. Everyone except for Mr. Downs was saved. But now, what you need is an explanation of what you saw." I had kind of already guessed what had happened, but I decided to play along.

"The man in the armor was Yuri Klatschnikov. He is one of Liebnitz's highest-ranking military commanders and one of the original circle that formed the organization. He was born in Russia but brought to Germany at an early age, so he has no trace of a Russian accent. He is highly dangerous and has a sometimes comical sense of humor. He was wearing a suit of shuritanium armor, which made him invulnerable to most forms of physical damage, apparently including our latest electromagnetic force fields. The suit had an embedded electrostatic field generator, which he used to shut down the system. The tanks and the jets were only there for show. If Klatschnikov had wanted, he could have blown the campus up by himself.

"The footage suggests that Liebnitz has ordered Klatschnikov to hunt you, making you a high-priority target.

He is probably searching for you right now. That is why we must accelerate your training, Pierre. To test if you have inherited your father's abilities and to what degree, you will be given a task and a set amount of time to complete it."

"Wait a second," I said, interrupting Mr. Roland, which took him aback. "You just said that shuritanium is *apparently* resistant to your electromagnetic force fields. I thought that the FBI vigorously tested all of its systems before putting them into the field? I'm sure that if you know about shuritanium, you must have some lying around. And also, when did I ever say I was randomly going to just jump onto the bandwagon and join your war effort? I'm at heart a stout pacifist."

Mr. Roland seemed to swell up for a few seconds, but he quickly calmed himself again. "First off, Pierre," he said in a quavering voice, "you will *not* talk to your superiors that way!" I jumped as he shouted the word *not.* "Second," he continued, "shuritanium is not a run-of-the-mill material that we can constantly use in field tests. As such, we were forced to make assumptions. Contrary to popular belief, the FBI is not an organization that possesses infinite resources. Finally, you were considered part of the war effort the moment you set foot on this base. That means I am your commanding officer and that you take orders without question. Is that clear?"

Clearly this was a battle I couldn't win, so I gave in. "Yes sir," I said. "Never mind what I just said, continue on." Mr. Roland instantly brightened up again as if I hadn't said anything. "Very well, then. Continuing on...

"Your task is to design a projectile that can penetrate a sheet of shuritanium and create a firearm that can hold the aforementioned projectile. Your goal is to do this as quickly as possible and with as few resources as possible. You will get information on the properties of shuritanium, and you will have our entire inventory at your disposal. You will start working once you arrive at our workshop. Any questions?"

"No sir," I replied. "Lead the way to the workshop." I followed Mr. Roland out of the room without acknowledging my dad. Once again we wound our way through the twisting corridors of the base, going farther and farther down into the earth. After a few minutes of rapid walking, we arrived at our destination.

A door slid open, and we stepped inside. The workshop was enormous, with a high, arched ceiling and long worktables with all sorts of tools and components lined up for me to work with. I saw the specs of shuritanium lying on one of the tables and headed over there. I was astounded by the sheer size of the room. Never had I had so many resources at my disposal before. It was amazing. Suddenly a question popped into my head. "No computer modeling, sir?" I asked. "Nope," replied Mr. Roland, "you'll do it all in your head this time." I replied, "Very well, sir."

I sat down and made myself comfortable, gathering the essential parts and tools that I needed. "Well," said Mr. Roland, "I'll leave you to it then. Someone will bring you food and water at periodic intervals, and a cot will be set up. Good luck, Pierre. You'll need it."

Mr. Roland wheeled away and headed for the door. Once he left, the door slid shut behind him, leaving me alone in the workshop with my thoughts and ideas.

4

The Meaning of Hate

Pierre Hartford

I began to sift through the mounds of parts and tools to see what I had. Laser saws, sonic welders, rocket-propelled screwdrivers…they really had given me the full set of tools. I also had some very rare parts, including turbocharged mega-jolts, L-tube energizers, wormhole dissipaters, and V-cube monoscropic vortex manipulators. I pulled out the specs for shuritanium.

I was impressed by the properties of the material. Very impressed indeed. I was worried, though, when I saw the amount of punishment a 250-atom-thick sheet can take considering that the armor Klatschnikov was wearing had to be at least six inches thick. A square nanometer of shuritanium can take thirty-five thousand pounds of force, which is amazing. It is also resistant to corrosion, has a melting point of six thousand degrees Celsius, is able to sustain its shape through an electromagnetic suppressor, and cannot be electrified. All of this multiplied by two billion and you can see my dilemma, especially when advanced computerized systems were built into the armor. But shuritanium cannot be electrified, and the FBI knew this, so why deploy an electromagnetic force field? Something was off, but I had to focus on the task at hand now.

Why though had I been given wormhole dissipaters and V-cube monoscropic vortex manipulators? These have no practical use as weaponry components. They can only be used in mini-teleporters like Mr. Roland's. They work by using massive amounts of energy to rip apart space and time and create a looped wormhole. To bring down the energy requirement to a minimal amount, though, the wormhole is stretched through the temporal dimension, which explains the aging backward to a certain point and then aging forward to the present. The time needed to go from one place to another is minimal. However, the size of the teleporters and their very high price prevent the widespread use of the technique.

Then came the turbocharged megajolts and L-tube energizers. These components store massive amounts of energy in very small volumes. This decreases the size of the teleporter, but the price is still prohibitively high. They had only created a device the size of a mask with turbocharged megajolts, so how had Mr. Roland transported us with a watch-sized teleporter?

That had to mean that they had solved the string theory for a unification of the forces—a theory of everything, the holy grail of physics. String theory states that the universe is actually made up of tiny vibrating strings; the strings make up particles and are vibrating in a space that has at least nine dimensions, with most dimensions curled into microscopic sizes. The four fundamental forces include the strong nuclear force, electromagnetism, the weak nuclear force, and gravity. The strong nuclear force involves fusion, which is a virtually limitless energy supply. Did that mean that the FBI had novel fusion technology running on a feedback loop that constantly replenished the energy supply of the megajolts?

I was beginning to grow suspicious of the FBI. The organization was very secretive, and the agents didn't let people into their inner circle unless they really needed them. They had solved two of the biggest problems of the century, yet they told nobody. How did they expect the world to trust them if they behaved this way? No wonder there was so much discord between countries—the human nature of suspicion. Wait a second...fusion technology? Energy source for teleportation parts?

Eureka! I had a possible solution! There must be fusion technology components in this heap of parts, and I could use the vortex manipulators and wormhole dissipaters to form a looping current that would allow movement through other dimensions and reappearance at another location in our universe. Yes! The turbocharged megajolts would hold the charge, the L-tube energizer would excite the charge, and voila! I would create a two-way teleportation system that allowed for signal transmission onto the bullet and the gun! This would defeat the purpose of shuritanium armor if the bullet could teleport straight into the heart of someone, theoretically. This weapon would obviously never be used...right?

While Pierre figured out a way to defeat the impenetrable properties of shuritanium, unbeknownst to him, there was a flicker of movement in a secluded corner of the workshop. A tiny beep was heard, and a device shut off. With a closer look, one could see that it was a camera with an attached thought-scanning device. Through the help of a transmitter, a person stared through the lens of the camera and read Pierre's thoughts.

This person wore black, as if at a funeral. His hair was blacker than the darkest night. He was covered in shadows. Habitually, his face wore a sadistic expression. The effect was amplified by the ugly scar disfiguring his handsome face, running across it like a spear. This person had unimaginable resources at his disposal. He was one of the most powerful men in the world. He reveled in a cloak of sadistic principles. Who was this man? Karl von Liebnitz.

Karl von Liebnitz

I leaned back as I shut off the camera and the thought scanner. The Hartford boy was just like his father, but he was young and full of untapped potential. I was lucky to even have a camera able to survey Pierre, but after all, *ich bin kein Dummkopf.* My NSA agent had placed it there many years ago, and no one had ever bothered to notice the camera and remove it. Just so that I would always know where to find that slimy, sniveling viper called Hartford. I could destroy them now if I wanted to. What joy it would bring me.

Nein, I cannot destroy them now. I must let the boy develop his skills to a manageable level of expertise. Once I buy that contemptible fool Roland, I will be able to foster the schism and drive the boy into my arms.

Klatschnikov is out there, searching. Let him search for a while more. It is scant punishment for the pain that has been inflicted on me. Klatschnikov failed to catch the Hartford boy, and he escaped my clutches. That must not happen again, or else. The boy can become my assistant, my right-hand lieutenant. I pride myself on being a much better mentor than the fools at the FBI. All because of Hartford. All because of him did this whole fiasco of Tyrannei brew into being in the first place. I closed my eyes and let the streams of the past bombard me.

Oh, if it could only be that I was *jung nochmal.* I would never befriend that poor boy who came up to me and broke my solitude. The problem was that we both had special intellectual gifts, and we both had a ruthless attitude. We fit together like two halves of a whole. Why then did he have to plant the seeds of envy in my heart and make me bring a new meaning to hate?

It really started when we went to our first competition together. We were both naive and young; he was eleven and I was six. It was a pool of 128 students. We were placed on opposite sides of the draw. We both easily destroyed all of the competition. We were the final two left in the competition. It was time for us to face each other. The task was to create and use a robot that could lift five tons. The task was simple. Whoever finished first would win.

I worked faster than Hartford, having a more pliable and creative mind. I was very close to being done, and he was further from the finish than I. Then his hypercompetitive spirit took over, making his next series of actions totally look like an accident. He fumbled with a wrench he was picking up, and it sailed into the air and hit my bucket of parts. My parts went flying everywhere and with them my final component. It was a microprocessor that I had programmed. It landed next to his wrench. He picked up the wrench and, in the process of doing that, stomped on the microprocessor, smashing it, and kicked it away into a mound of bolts. I was shocked. I scrambled over to his workstation and started frantically looking for the microprocessor, scooping up parts in the process. By the time I found it, Hartford had finished. The judge said that Hartford had unintentionally caused an "accident," so he was not disqualified and won the trophy.

When we were out of sight of the judge, I began screaming at his face, asking why he had cheated to win. He calmed me down with the crummy excuse of an accident. I calmed down, but Hartford had already shown his true nature; the seeds were planted and growing.

In the next competition, we were in the final again, and I made sure to pay back the favor. Again it was ruled an "accident," and I won. He grew incensed with me and demanded an apology. I said sorry and left. The seeds grew bigger. I understood unfairness. This was an unfair relationship. I endured it, however, because I had no one else.

In the competitions thereafter, there were often "accidents" because we always faced off in the finals. We both won sometimes, but Hartford won more often. Our bond was fracturing, but I still hung on. Then came the news from MIT.

There was one opening available, and we both had a chance. It turned into a fierce competition between us. Sometimes he had the upper hand; sometimes I had it. It was obvious, though, that I was smarter even though I was only thirteen. The balance went both ways. Then came the reply. Hartford was accepted; I was not. We both knew that I had the better mind and that I should have gotten the spot. My patience snapped, and the bond disintegrated. I screamed at Hartford, releasing my pent-up fury and anger into his face. He had the nerve to jab back.

Our friendship was a shambles. I turned around and walked away, ending that chapter of my life. I learned later that my robot sent to MIT had been sabotaged because the microchips Hartford had given me were defective. I had my proof by putting two and two together.

I wandered around, my soul shattered by that callous fool, planning my sweet and delicious revenge. I came upon the idea to form an organization, led by yours truly, to conquer the world and cleanse it of disease, creating a holy empire. With my intellectual weapons, I could equip my recruits and earn a steady income to annex the countries of the world.

I acted upon this idea. I wandered the streets for what seemed like days on end. Finally I found Yuri Klatschnikov. He was the perfect man to recruit others. I brought him onto my side and convinced him of the viability of my plan. We were kindred souls, filled with the same sentiments against the world. Klatschnikov recruited a few more core members, including Bartleby and Joubert. Klatschnikov brought them in by the dozen, and they brought dozens more with them. The ranks of Tyrannei swelled up. I kept myself hidden and developed the organization.

I heard of Hartford's success at Cybor and placed the

doddering Gurov to spy there as a "scientist." He brought back
reams of useless information, trickles that were useful. I set
up my spy network around the world. I trained my soldiers
to become mindless killing machines. I developed outlandish
technology.

Then I introduced myself to the world. I hacked the invulnerable networks and revealed my master plan. I wish I could
have seen Hartford's face when he saw what I had become
because of his stupidity. I began my assault. First, I annexed
das Vaterland, deposing Merkel III and installing a puppet to
rule. I used the new resources at hand to expand Tyrannei and
become stronger.

I became a demigod in the eyes of the world. Resources
went toward stopping my outward expansion, which dissolved
uselessly in front of their eyes. All of the money…gone to
waste and willingly donated. I was happy in my current state.

Then Gurov retrieved a useful piece of information. He
had "invented" a strange new eye implant, the Eye Spy 0.2. I
looked at the specs for the device and immediately saw the unbridled potential of the product were I to conquer the source.
I told Gurov my new plan to conquer Cybor. I didn't know,
after all, that he had been compromised by Hartford. I wanted
Hartford to die painfully.

That was my key mistake—that and not eliminating Gurov
before the coup took place. I expected Hartford not to foresee
the date and fight back. And when he did not, I was happy but
suspicious. Hartford, however, was already off the map. My
men came up with nothing. I was content. I took over Cybor
mit den Puppen and improved the Eye Spy, issuing it to my men.
I also developed shuritanium during that time period.

Only two weeks ago did I realize my follies, and they were brutal and almost fatal. They could be rectified though, and that plan was ready to swing into action. It was—

"Meister," said a voice through the intercom. I snapped out of my meditation and saw the face of my secretary on the video feed. "*Da ist ein Anruf von Klatschnikov,*" she replied. I muttered bitterly under my breath and took the call. Klatschnikov's face appeared. "Meister," he said. "*Da ist keine Spur—*"

An alarm started blaring. System corrupted. System corrupted. I engaged my electromagnetic field. The system turned off as the electromagnetic field fried the entire grid. The alarm stopped. Another mistake of mine. The question here was not what or why, but how. How had Hartford hacked the system and planted a devious bug? This was a supposedly unhackable system. Finally I had a problem to solve. If Hartford unnerved me, I could unnerve him as well. He would see...

5

THE GAUNTLET IS PICKED UP

Through the holotransmitters, the State of the Union news broadcast of the 324th day of 2067 was moved up to a special time slot of 1500 hours. As the broadcast began, so too did the news anchor's steady drone.

"Welcome to today's edition of State of the Union," mumbled the news anchor. "Today we have breaking news that MIT has apparently been razed to the ground by radical jihadists. The president of MIT was killed; everyone else escaped. The terrorists proceeded to bomb the campus. Apparently, the specially designed defense system was taken down by an electrostatic field, which is supposed to be impossible to do. For more on this breaking event, we go now to our technical correspondent for details on how the system could have been disabled."

The screens switched to a man with a buzz cut. "Hello," he said gruffly. "The MIT defense system was custom designed and employed various advanced technologies. That system included an electromagnetic disruptor shield, laser stun guns, rocket launchers, ice beams, disassembling bullet sponges, and automatic ballistic missiles. I am sure you are familiar with most of these technologies, as simpler versions are on the market. You may not know, however, what a disassembling bullet sponge is. This is a piece of equipment that can absorb large amounts of damage. It also can be disassembled by an automatic laser gearshift when there is too much damage. These parts will continue to absorb extensive damage, slowing the enemy down.

"The electromagnetic disruptor shield was created to defeat the new electrostatic fields that can shut down defense systems. It could absorb an energy surge of up to forty-five thousand gigajoules. However, a set of armor with cutting-edge technologies, which would render it invulnerable to all modern electrification techniques, could walk straight through the shield and destroy one of the shield generators hooked to the defense system, rendering the entire defense useless.

"The reason the defense system was shut down so easily is that a certain terrorist exposed the electromagnetic disruptor shield to an energy surge of approximately ninety thousand gigajoules, which should be theoretically impossible using current technology. This man also wore an impenetrable suit of armor that prevented him from being shot down by the defenses. This meant that the system could quite effectively be shut down."

The broadcast switched back to the news anchor. "Now let's hear what the president has to say about this latest development," he droned. The screen showed the president giving a speech. "Ladies and gentlemen," he began. "Yesterday, one of our finest engineering schools, the Massachusetts Institute

of Technology, was attacked. The attackers, apparently jihadists, disabled the defense system and then razed the campus.
Mr. Downs, the esteemed president of the university, was pro-
nounced dead. Although the students were evacuated safely,
we lost a gem of our engineering indus—"

The broadcast suddenly blacked out. The screens turned
black and failed. After a few seconds, they came back online.
Once the start-up routine was over, however, the news broadcast was no longer being shown. Instead there was a picture of
the presidential palace.

As words appeared on the screens, a man spoke with a
clipped accent. "Hello, puppet states of the North American
continent. This is a message for your chief, the one whom they
call the president." On the screens, a picture of the president
appeared. "By now, you must all have heard of the sad destruction of MIT." The screens now showed MIT being blown to
bits. "Well, I am here to tell you that we, the Tyrannei, are re-
sponsible for the attack. I, Karl von Liebnitz, ordered it." The
screens showed the emblem of a double-edged sword on fire,
superimposed on an image of Liebnitz. "The message for your
president is as follows: We have thrown down the gauntlet.
The ball is in your court. You can surrender the boy, Pierre
Hartford, whom the precious FBI is keeping hidden, and we
will cease our attacks on your puny empire. Or you can pick up
the gauntlet, thereby declaring war on the Tyrannei, which you
will brutally lose. Your choice, President. You have forty-eight
hours to reply."

The screens showed MIT blowing up again, and then
the screens blacked out. The news report came back onto
the screens, with the anchor looking shocked and shaken up.

"We…we…well," he stammered, "I thi…think we will cut the pro…gra…gram short today. Until to…mo…morrow." The news anchor began to sob as the screens turned black again.

Inside the presidential palace, the president sat with a shocked expression on his face, newly teleported inside. He did not even know who this Hartford boy was. Perhaps he was unimportant and he could avoid hostilities by giving up the boy, whoever he was. But Liebnitz needed to be repaid for his impudence. Well, he would make his decision after calling Christian and asking him who Pierre Hartford was.

"Mr. Burns," he called to his secretary, "phone Mr. Roland for me and tell him I want to talk about the Hartford boy." The call was made and the video screen flared to life. On the screen, however, was not Mr. Roland but rather Will Hartford. "Mr. President," he said tonelessly. "Will Hartford," replied the president. "Where is Mr. Roland? I would like to talk to him privately."

"If it is about my son, I think you will find that I can answer your questions more readily than Mr. Roland," replied Will. "I *said* I would like to talk to Mr. Roland," replied the president with a sharp note in his voice. "Very well, *sir*," replied Will with a touch of venom. He got up and went to find Mr. Roland.

Will Hartford

I walked away from the main office disgusted at our *most honorable majestic emperor who calls himself president of the United States.* As I had told Pierre, the world had to be cleansed of

corruption. The only problem was that Karl and I found ourselves on opposite sides of the divide. We were both utterly
without scruples, ruthless killers. Why did I have to have a son
blessed with strict moral values? Why?

There were some things I had not told Pierre for fear of
his even greater horrific reaction. As it was, I had already
fragmented the bond. But at least I had not told him of our
cheater's exploits, our hidden animosities, and my arrogant,
high-handed behavior that caused him to lose it. I was, after
all, guilty as well. We both knew perfectly well that although
we were both among the smartest people in the world, Karl
had a sharper creativity and intellect than I did. But he also
had the flaw of hubris, of which I was fortunately spared.

Oh, what we could have done together. But we worked
toward the same goal on opposite sides of the divide. I would
not be as brutal as he though. If he won, all hope was lost. The
oppressor of the ages would come to light.

But I had to fix things with Pierre after he figured out the
shuritanium conundrum. The schism would drive apart the
whole cause. First, the president had to declare war. At least I
had prepared a little surprise for Karl, something that would
anger him to the extreme: my very own bug to corrupt his system, making him waste an hour shutting down his system and
debugging it, while giving us more time. After all, he knew
how to debug rapidly, but this was no regular bug.

Karl von Liebnitz

I muttered under my breath, hating that stuck-up idiot
Hartford more with every passing second. This would just be,

after all, another nuisance that would take five minutes to fix. I hurried up and reached the main power grid. I pulled out a portable clamp and my G-boost debugger and clamped the debugger onto one of the power streams, which were inactive as the system was being rebooted.

When the system came back online to restore power to one stream, the lines of code rolled down my screen. Suddenly the machine began to beep rapidly. I became confused. Debuggers were not programmed to beep rapidly. Then I saw the screen. It said in red letters: *overload*. I threw the debugger across the grid and it shattered. Hartford had planted a surface under-bug crawler during the broadcast. That meant scanning every line of code and debugging it, costing me fifty-five minutes and letting them talk without me monitoring them. Perhaps I should not have tried to hack all of the holostreams. After all, the majority would have been watching the State of the Union. I had been overconfident…again.

I went back to my office and began the slow, onerous task of looking through every single line of code in the system, blaming myself all the more for my slovenliness.

Christian Roland

I finally had a few moments to relax. After all, having my job meant getting absolutely no rest at all. Now, however, Pierre and Will were busy, and the other personnel knew better than to bother me.

Suddenly, however, Will walked into my room. In a clipped tone, he said, "There is a call waiting for you from the *president of the United States*, sir." I shot up and groaned inwardly. Just when I had some peace, the president had to come along and break up my rest time. You have to be kidding me. I hurried up and arrived at the headquarters.

On the big vidscreen, the worn-out face of the president stared back. I grew nervous. The president would only call if something big had happened. Right when I was not on duty, there had to be some sort of spying going on. "What happened, Mr. President?" I asked worriedly. "You've got to be kidding me, Christian," replied the president with a sarcastic laugh. "You did not just miss what happened, right?" I sighed inwardly. "They always seem to do something during my fifteen minutes of rest, sir," I replied. "Fill me in on the details."

"Well," replied the president, "I need to ask you about Hartford's son, Pierre." My heart sank like a stone. Liebnitz was moving fast. He was throwing down a gauntlet to the president. The war was already beginning. Shoot. Our bases would have to be prepared. "Let me guess," I replied. "Liebnitz sent you a message: declare war or give us Pierre and we will spare you."

"Something along those lines," replied the president. "So I have to ask you, how important is Pierre to the American cause? What will be the consequences of giving him up? I need to know before I send back my reply." I answered without a second of hesitation. "Declare war, sir," I replied. "Don't even hesitate for a second. Pierre is our one and only hope of winning. You give him Pierre, and he's won. Pierre has the potential to be more than his father ever was and will be. Pierre is much bigger than you would care to think, sir."

"Very well," replied the president. "I guess that it has come to war with the Tyrannei. Let us hope for the best, Christian. I have a feeling that he has more than a few tricks up his sleeve waiting to trip us up. But everything would have come to this point sooner or later anyway. I guess the time has come."

"I wish you the best of luck, sir," I replied. "I have my own preparations to make concerning our bases. As you prepare the military, I will send you the shock troopers. Goodbye, sir."

The call shut off. I sighed, feeling tired, old, and defeated. This war would sap all of our strength. Pierre was the hinge on which the fate of the world rested. Hopefully he could live up to the expectations. I would assume, however, that first the dog Klatschnikov would be sent to attack us, for Liebnitz would organize the war. So then…oh, shoot. Liebnitz controlled MIT. Downs couldn't have taken the vault files in the hydro-decaying lock chamber. That lock was sealed with a specialized pressure container that contained a decaying unit of radioactive water. If Liebnitz found those files, it was all over. He already knew about this base, but then he would find out everything. Well, I guess this was our chance to train Pierre to win the war for us by bringing back the files.

6

EUREKA!

Pierre Hartford

Finally. After a couple of grueling hours, I had painstakingly completed my hand-drawn schematics of my prototypical teleporting bullet weapon. I was positive that all of the parts I wanted would be somewhere in the mound of parts and in the quantities required. I began by taking out the rare parts I needed because they could be crushed when I sifted through the bolted cylindrical metalloid gyroscopes and other disturbingly large quantities of bulky parts. If only I could spread these parts over a wide area and sort them without having to look through this morass. I sighed.

Suddenly I felt as if a hidden switch had been turned on in my mind. I looked back at the pile with a newfound understanding of the hidden properties of the buried parts and their locations. I looked directly at a regular spherical connector, and I could see everything that was affecting the sphere—and I mean everything. I saw the wind pressure, the amount of gravitational force pushing it down, and so on.

I willed the sphere to float off the worktable by endeavoring to fine-tune the gravitational field with my mind. My God! This was amazing! The sphere actually floated a foot off the table! I set it back down with some carelessness, and it banged into the table with a clang and made a small dent.

Now came the big test. I attempted to extend the tendrils of my mind to seep into every part in the pile. When I was pretty sure that I had manifested my consciousness into most of the parts, I made all of the parts hover simultaneously. I nudged the parts with spurts of air to spread them far apart. Now I had to sort the parts. I bent the magnetic fields ever so slightly to let the electric fields charge the specific types of parts differently. Then I concentrated on curling a magnetic field around one of each type of part. I let the main magnetic field dissipate, and the parts sorted themselves by zooming through the air to the magnet with the opposite charge. Success!

I looked back down at the schematics I had drawn and assembled the prototype inside my head. Without consciously thinking about it, the parts I needed flew toward me and each other. In a matter of minutes, the parts had built themselves into my prototypical weapon. What should have taken me days had only taken an hour to complete. I was stunned by the sudden broadening of my mind. Undoubtedly I had some sort of telekinesis through a neural circuit that should have remained dormant inside my brain. Eureka! I screamed the word out loud, and it rebounded through the room.

Now I could test the weapon. I levitated a table into a

vertical position and reinforced it by assembling a ramshackle shield. I loaded my weapon and fired a bullet at the table. It struck the shield and did not penetrate it. I loaded my weapon again and fired. This time, though, milliseconds before the bullet would hit the shield, I unconsciously slowed down time. The bullet appeared to be moving oh so slowly now. I pressed another button on the weapon. Time sped back up to normalcy. The bullet vanished into thin air! I pressed another button a second or two later. The bullet reappeared, flying toward the far wall. I leaped through the air with joy. I ran a victory lap around a table. As I came back around, I ran toward the door, shouting Mr. Roland's name. I mentally ripped the door off its hinges in my excitement and sprinted through the halls to find Mr. Roland.

Karl von Liebnitz

I would murder Hartford later if I missed some important things during my debugging of his stupid surface underbug crawler. I rapidly analyzed the code line by line, quickly correcting the bugged areas. Why were there fifty-six million lines of code needed to power this facility? That was obviously because *I* had written every single bit of it. Unfortunately, Bartleby and his men were useless at debugging code. I debugged their code for them after they had written some more hacking software. No elegance in their syntax either. At least I could telekinetically reach through the computer and quickly power the keys to complete what physical flesh would have taken hours or even days to do.

I sighed and went back to work. I expected a declaration of

war pretty soon. Perhaps the so-called president would try to bluff his way into the inevitability of having a plausible reason to declare war, in addition to what I had fed him. Anyway, Roland would soon be my man for the taking. He was stupid enough to leave himself vulnerable to a hostage crisis.

I sighed. At least the robots didn't care if they died. I could already see the bloody and brutal war that would start before my eyes. This would become World War IV, but not before I quelled the superpower that could provide the resources to put me down with help from the other nations. The president would have his hands tied when it came to finding allies for his suicidal plunge into the unknown.

They were all tied up in diplomatic red tape anyway, bound by their petty little trade obligations. They could all be manipulated through their obsessive desire for their Eye Spy implants. Just get the transmitter networks online in time and the war would be over. The president would lose all guise of public support. Even his petty Congress full of hot air balloons would be helpless against the poor masses.

Oh, *der alte* Karl still had a few tricks up his sleeve. New recruits, a new army, new weaponry…the list spanned about five pages of jumbo-sized holographic transmissions. I knew how to hack the networks by now. Their firewalls were so porous that I could have poured a cup of milk through without any of it remaining on my side of the wall. It was ridiculous to say the least.

If only I could take Hartford out of the picture and shut him off in his tiny digital cell with no hope of using his rebooting system. To do that, I would have to build a bug so sophisticated that it would look identical to some of the code he was using to do his work, among it the bug hacking my network—

Wait a second. I had some of Hartford's code in my system right now. His surface underbug crawler. I could easily rerig it to sneak into his system and break it down, which he wouldn't be able to prevent. But I was erasing the bug from my system even now. *Warte, nein!* Stop! I wrenched my mind to a halt. Luckily I hadn't debugged the whole system during my meditation and kept a trash bin of bugs and codes that my lazy technician periodically emptied.

"Hey, Foligno!" I snapped across the room. "Give me the code I started deleting forty-three minutes ago. Take it out of the trash bin, and put it back into the system in an isolated firewall." "Ja, Meister," he replied. He started clacking away at his keyboard like mad. Soon I had the bug back and finished storing it. Eureka! Watch your own poison come back and bite you now, snake!

Christian Roland

I sighed and leaned back in my chair. Liebnitz moved too fast. He wanted to catch us off guard, I realized. He assumed that Pierre would take a month or two to develop his potential. Hopefully that wouldn't be the case. If he developed too late and we couldn't untangle ourselves from the red tape and mobilize our allies, we were all dead meat.

I was considering this turn of events as Pierre burst in. "Mr. Roland, sir," he shouted. "I've done it! I've done it! The switch has flipped! I was handwriting my schematics for a few hours, and then I realized I needed to sort and spread the parts out, and a switch flipped in my brain, and I manipulated the stuff using my brain, and it moved and I sorted it, and then the gun built itself, and the test was successful, sir!" The words just spilled out of the excited young man's mouth, flowing like a river that couldn't be held back. "Pierre," I responded calmly, "I'm glad that you're excited, but I need you to calm down and speak to me so I can understand exactly what you're trying to tell me." Pierre visibly calmed down and looked ashamed. "Sorry, sir," he said. "I'll explain what happened."

Pierre gave me an account of what had happened in the workshop. I was amazed by his stunningly detailed and peculiar account of events. "You're telling me, Pierre," I said slowly and with awe in my voice, "that you managed to manipulate both the object and the field itself?" Pierre replied, "Yes sir." I asked, "You also managed to come up with an amazingly ingenious and advanced weapon in a matter of hours?" Again he answered, "Yes sir."

I jumped and, with an ecstatic look on my face, I went and embraced Pierre in a bear hug. "Yes, Pierre!" I shouted, with tears streaming down my face. "You've done it in record time! Ha! Take that, Tyrannei!" Then I began to think rationally again. "Pierre," I beseeched him, "show me a demonstration, for the love of God!" He concentrated and a book on defensive trenches floated off my desk. The object was manipulated. Now a demonstration of the field was needed.

Suddenly some of the small metal objects in the room flew toward a spot in midair and stuck to each other. Just as rapidly, the objects flew back to their initial positions. I was truly and utterly satisfied. I shouted, "Eureka!" and ran into the hall toward the coding room and Will Hartford. Eureka! We had a slight edge now, especially if Liebnitz was debugging because of the hacking that Will had done. Eureka!

I nearly ran into Will, who had come out to see what the ruckus was all about. "What's happened to make you cry tears of joy, Christian?" Will asked confusedly. "Your son," I said, panting for breath, "has unprecedented skills and potential. He can already manipulate with great skill and invent very advanced objects quite rapidly. He can control not only the objects but also the fields themselves. Will, do you understand now?" Will looked at me in shock. "He can control the fields?" he spluttered. "But that's an unprecedented feat! We have the edge! Ha! Take that, you hubristic idiot!" Will ran over and hugged me. Eureka! We were truly over the top this time.

Oh, if only Will Hartford and Christian Roland had known. A certain man called Agent Hirschel, one of the personal bodyguards, had slipped through during their careful selection. He had been a spy all along for Karl von Liebnitz, and he nearly burst into tears of joy himself when he saw that he had recorded the entire conversation between Roland and the Hartford snake. What a gold mine for his Meister! The fools had played right into his hands. The joy of outsmarting one of the most brilliant minds of the century to help one even more brilliant! The war would truly be over before it even began, in his opinion.

7

THE HUMBLE BEGINNINGS
OF A FLAME

Karl von Liebnitz

Finally, my system was back online and debugged. Hartford's code was stored away for future use. All could go back to normal now. More preparations had to be made for the imminent war. I sighed and sat back. Should I just make the war short but glorious, or should I give them false hope, only to make the loss all the crueler for them?

Suddenly Agent Hirschel's special number flashed before my eyes, indicating an incoming message. He was a useful, if not crucial, spy. "Meister," he stated simply, "I have very important messages." I could tell he was trying to contain his building bubble of excitement. Ha-ha! Hartford's bug hadn't stopped me from learning anything important!

"Display the messages, Bradley," I replied calmly.

Hirschel's face disappeared, and sound waves appeared on the screen with labels indicating the people behind the voices. I listened to the first recording with a sigh of disappointment. The president was behaving as expected. Roland was playing into my trap.

Then the last recording began. I listened to it in its entirety and replayed it several times. It had video footage as well. I sat back, shocked to my very core. Pierre was developing that fast? My plan of surprise was already cracking at the seams. And I could not manipulate the forces now as he could as a complete novice! The boy was amazing and already developing his mental powers at twenty-one. He was a much bigger asset than I would have ever expected. Hartford's arrogance made me chuckle. I needed that boy before they could deploy him.

I called Klatschnikov, and he appeared on the implanted neural screen. "Yuri," I asked, "where are you?" He shrugged. "Searching for the base in the Gobi Desert, Meister," came his reply. "I know where the base is, Yuri." Klatschnikov twitched unconsciously. "*Was?*" he shouted. "How long have you known?" I laughed internally at his lost composure. "Your punishment for letting the Hartford boy escape, Yuri. You've been conducting a useless search. I've known that for quite a while."

Klatschnikov was fuming. "That was *not* my fault, Meister. Where is the base then?" He forced the words out through gritted teeth. I smiled. "In the Mojave Desert, dear Commander," I replied. "Here are the coordinates." I scanned the coordinates and sent them through my neural transmitter. "Attack on my command," I added. "The war must begin in a coordinated fashion." I cut off the connection before Klatschnikov could reply.

Yuri Klatschnikov

I was about to reply to Meister's dry, cutting comments when he cut off the connection. I screamed out loud and gritted my teeth. The shuritanium armor appeared as I spread my arms, and I shot at the sand dunes, raising clouds of sand into the air. I was Meister's first recruit. I was the one who comforted him after he had abandoned Hartford.

Still, Meister was merciless. He cared for nothing but himself and his goals, using everyone as pawns. He was emotionless, sly, and cunning. Even I got punished for failure in the most humiliating manner possible.

I had only been a disillusioned teenager, just like Meister. That was how we had bonded in the first place. I thought back, protected by my shuritanium shell, and allowed to show true emotion only in that protective enclosure.

I was sixteen when I found Meister. My parents had uprooted me from Mother Russia and brought me to Merkel's German Dumpster at age five, setting up my unhappy and disillusioned childhood. They had made me into a maniacal clown, giving me a twisted sense of humor. Oh, they had paid for it with their lives.

My day had been like any other day. When I was walking through the dark alleys after school, I saw a thirteen-year-old boy sobbing uncontrollably against a wall. I walked by him, ignoring him, when some tendril of thought pulled me back to stand in front of him, leaving me bewildered.

"Can I help you?" I asked in a kind way, surprised that I wasn't forcing the words out of my mouth. "Nein," he muttered quickly. "You are in a bad way though, my good sir," I replied, astonishing myself more than him. He looked up with newfound hostility. "Stop offering me fake sympathy, idiot," he snarled. I jumped back, astonished by his outburst.

I tried a different approach. "You and I are kindred spirits," I said cautiously. The boy looked up at me. "How so?" he asked disdainfully. "We are both disillusioned souls, looking for an uncorrupted place to be in peace." I wondered how I knew this. It was as if the right thoughts were being placed inside my head and coming out of my mouth. "We hate the current authorities and would like to form a new government where we can cleanse the world from the cancer. Don't you see? We can combine our hatreds and form an organization that will stand against this porous pillar of authority."

The boy looked at me, astonished, but that was nothing compared to my astonishment. Some spirit must be taking me over to make me talk and feel in this strange manner. "You have some very good ideas, *Freund*," he said softly. My heart jumped. We were friends. "I think we should find some other disillusioned souls and implement your plan," he continued. "Then we can institute our reformation of the world."

"Ja, Freund," was my excited reply. "We will create an organization to reshape the world and cleanse the diseased pores." I extended my hand. He shook it. "Let us meet again tomorrow," he said, "in this alley, at this corner." I shook my head. "No," I replied, "I'll take you home with me. Then we can talk." At home, we formed Tyrannei. The seed had been planted.

I snapped back to the actual time and place and was astonished to find glimmering, pearly tears rolling down my face. Meister had rewarded me, but he did not really care for me. Perhaps he cared more for that fool Bartleby. I was the one who had planted Tyrannei into his mind. He had declared himself the leader. I had stood by him without a complaint. Perhaps it was time to branch off on my own. No! I snapped the unruly thought in half and banished it out of my head.

The shuritanium armor folded back up. I called my battalion together, and we prepared to break camp and head to the coordinates Meister had given me. Hopefully the sentries at MIT were not letting their guard down.

Pierre Hartford, before the time frame in the above section

Mr. Roland came back with Father, a radiant smile starting on one face and ending on the other. They really were happy. And I didn't even know how I had these skills. "Congratulations," said Father, smiling benevolently at me. I stubbornly kept my mouth tightly shut.

Mr. Roland cleared his throat. "Now that you have developed your talents, Pierre," he said, "your father and I will be going with you on your first mission in the field. It shouldn't be too hard. We'll be heading back to MIT." I reflexively stiffened. "*No.*" I spat out the monosyllable, choking back tears. "Pierre," said Mr. Roland comfortingly, "I know how you feel about this, but this needs to happen. We need you to take out Liebnitz's men guarding MIT."

"Why?" I muttered. "There are some very secure and important files hidden inside a vault with a hydro-decaying lock that I just reset to open about the time we'll arrive at MIT. Even Mr. Downs didn't know the details of these files. They are from before his time. We're going to be taking a Mach 15 Turbojet because the files are, um, hard to carry," replied Mr. Roland.

I was impressed. At least we would travel in style. If there were important files that needed rescuing, I would of course agree to go and help the cause. I just had one question. "How do you want me to take out the men?" I asked. "Does this have any killing involv—" Mr. Roland cut me short. "No, no," he said quickly. "Liebnitz's men are outfitted with implants. Use them as focal points, utilizing electromagnetic fields to unbalance their emotions and make them fall asleep. No lasting damage." He smiled quickly.

"All right then," I said. "Let's go." Mr. Roland smiled. "Perfect," he said. "We just need to get outfitted, and we'll be ready." Mr. Roland walked out of the room with Father. I followed. We took winding paths upstairs until we reached a large room. "This is the armory and our main storage room," announced Mr. Roland.

Rows upon rows of weapons and armor stood stacked against one wall, making my mouth fall open in awe. Shredded barrels, reverse-engineered bullets, stacked mines, energized pulse seekers...there was just so much stuff!

Just by thinking about the weaponry, armor and weapons flew toward me and placed themselves on me in the perfect positions. Mr. Roland and Father watched in awe. Suddenly they were outfitted as well! My mind was subconsciously processing my thoughts and knew what I wanted to do before I would even think about it. Wow. The armor I was wearing folded itself up and turned into thick shoulder pads.

Mr. Roland had his jaw open about six inches. When I looked at him, he quickly closed it. "Wha—?" he managed to sputter. I replied in a nonchalant fashion. "Oh, I didn't really have to think about what to do, sir. Ever since that switch was flicked on in my mind, the forces manipulate themselves subconsciously when I need them to. It's simply amazing. I have no control over what's happening, and I wouldn't want to control this good talent even if I could."

I decided to give the ball back to Mr. Roland. "What kind of armor is this?" I asked him. "This isn't shuritanium, that's for sure." Mr. Roland looked at me queerly. "Can't you tell?" he asked. "It's vringarated blastoid clerium. This is the alternative material the FBI developed after failing to obtain a large supply of shuritanium. We do have some extra armor as well, equipped with all the weapons you'll need."

Mr. Roland went over to the roof and pulled a crank. The roof opened up, revealing an airfield with our jet waiting for us. The storage compartment opened as well as the boarding ramp of the beautiful aerial machine. Mach 15. Unbelievably fast.

Then Mr. Roland opened one of the thick metal boxes that were stacked against the other three sides of the room. "Ah, good," he said, pulling out a paper folder. "These are the correct files." I looked shocked. "You have paper files?!" I asked incredulously. "Those are so old!"

"Old, Pierre, but highly valuable," reprimanded Mr. Roland softly. "Now put all the boxes in the storage area of the aircraft." The boxes floated out of the room and into the jet.

"Very well, Pierre," said Mr. Roland. "By doing this, we are declaring war. Are you prepared for the consequences of your actions?" I thought for a second. "Yes sir," I replied slowly. "Very well, Pierre," said Mr. Roland. "War it is."

Klatschnikov was careful after MIT had been razed. Minesweepers had been sent into the ruins to check for traps and to disable the defenses for good. Handpicked men had been chosen to guard the place in case the United States Army would be sent in to take back MIT. They were meticulously careful and were experts at playing keep-away with expensive armies.

However, they did not know that there was a hidden hydro-decaying lock chamber, slowly ticking away the hours until it would open, just recently reset by the FBI. If they found the chamber and saw the files, the Americans would be wiped off the map.

One of the sentries laughed and began to eat his rations. "You think we will have anything to do tonight, Lars?" he asked his Norwegian companion. The Norwegian shrugged. "The Americans aren't declaring war yet, and why would they? They might try to get back their 'gem of an industry' later though. Ha-ha, tough luck for those fools." Lars laughed with a hearty guffaw.

His companion spat onto the ground and pulled a metal rod out of his pocket. He tossed it into the air, and a mechanism unraveled the rod and converted it into a buzzing scepter. "Wait till they see this beauty," said the companion. "They'll be so shocked that they'll lose their minds and run to their commanders screaming of demons." Lars and his companion both laughed.

Suddenly, however, the men began to feel sleepy and angry, becoming mentally unbalanced by the changing electromagnetic fields. They, along with the other guards, fell to the ground like dominoes. Their entire weaponry system shut itself down as the electromagnetic fields increased in strength because the guards were just that: guards, not technicians who could fix the flaw in the weaponry system. Pierre was doing a magnificent job for a novice in battle.

A ship appeared out of the sky with a ripple, and a few figures scampered out and floated to the ground. One of them was Pierre. After touching down, a weapon molded into his hand. He went off into the distance as a blur, searching for the chamber. Will and Mr. Roland followed, surprised by the manipulation of time demonstrated by Pierre.

8

A Nasty Surprise

Will Hartford

OK, this was unbelievable. Pierre was simply amazing as a novice, doing things effortlessly that had taken me a decade to learn. His mind was hot-wired to respond to his inputs before they reached the surface of his brain. I don't think that this was all because of Pierre having me as a father. There had to be some other factor involved.

But Pierre was not manipulating the objects as Karl and I had; he was manipulating the external forces around the fields. Technically Pierre was a paradox that should not have existed. Force field manipulation is an ability that can cause the brain to fry itself from overstraining of the neural bonds. However, he stood before us, and we had to maximize his potential and seize the opportunity.

To get some greater analysis though, I had to see him with

his weapon and run a battery of tests on him. If he could manipulate time and inhibit the emotional forces—not just the electromagnetic forces and gravity—then he, and we as an extension, would truly be an unstoppable juggernaut.

Wait...I hadn't told Christian some of the mechanics of the actual teleportation. Christian wasn't the original Christian anymore. The teleportation only opens atom-sized wormholes. The light scanned Christian down into atoms and rebuilt him on the other side with the information content. However, minor errors are sometimes caused by this mode of teleportation. There is a chance that anybody who travels through a wormhole can come out the other end drastically different, for even small errors can cause big changes.

Did that mean Pierre could have been an accident caused by a wormhole error? But then he'd have to be kept away from any and all wormholes. Unfortunately, Pierre was probably heading for a surprise. I bet you everything I owned that Karl had already set up something to trap us at MIT.

Christian Roland

Um, OK. Pierre was just...simply...amazing. That his subconscious mind was depriving him of a sort of free will was fine with me if he could just use his manipulative powers in that nonchalant manner. But they had just developed, according to Will. So how did Pierre have such control over the objects he thought about, much less the fields?

The real test would be if Pierre could manipulate every single force as well as time. If he could just slow that juggernaut and control the rates around certain areas with and without people in them, we would be unbeatable. If he could reverse time, well, let's just say that history would be unsafe to write.

There was just one thing that concerned me. Pierre said that it seemed as if a switch had been flipped on in his brain. Did that mean he was not completely human? Was he such a good robot I couldn't tell the difference? Or did that mean he could have his powers deactivated as well if one flipped the switch back to its off position? I felt as if something was being hidden from me. What was Will hiding?

Well, I had become used to people hiding things from me my entire life. But I was being hypocritical. As the chief of the FBI, I hid things from people all the time. My entire childhood had been one big fat manufactured fraud. I had lived in a seemingly normal "family" and had been a happy boy. However, there were certain eccentricities that befuddled me. Strange people came to visit and asked me weird questions. My "parents" would not answer my entreaties for an explanation.

One particularly poignant encounter summed up the strangeness of my childhood. One day a strange woman came to visit me. She brought me to my bedroom and pulled up a chair while I sat on my bed. We stared each other in the eyes for several long minutes. I finally lost my patience and blurted out, "Excuse me, but why are you just staring at me?" The woman jerked up and looked frazzled.

"Nothing to worry about, dear," she replied quickly. "That was just our way of introducing each other. Now I would like to ask you some questions." I wondered what kind of an introduction staring at me was. Interesting. "Are these the same questions from last week and the week before that and the week before that?" I whined. "They're so annoying." The woman sighed. "Christian, don't worry. The answers to these questions are important for me to hear week after week. They tell me a lot more about you than you could tell me."

I wondered how that was possible. How could she know more about me than I did? This question popped into my mind every time. "Christian," began the woman, "if I walked away from you, what would you do?" I replied with the same answer I had given the time before and the time before that: "I would let you walk away to cope with your emotions and see if you would come back." The woman continued with the same barrage of questions they all asked: What if she attacked me? What if I had information that she wanted? What if we were enemies and I had a choice between killing her or extracting information from her?

On and on it went in this fashion. I answered automatically, letting my mind fall into a dull stupor. Suddenly, however, I was jerked out of my stupor by a new question I did not expect. It was completely unrelated and made me think for a long time. I replied slowly but surely. "If I were put into such a position, I would let it die rather than save it for the future." Who would want to save corruptness?

The woman stood up abruptly and left. "Thank you for your time, Christian," she said. The door slammed shut behind her, leading me into a new part of my life. The next day, I was taken away to a secret facility. I never saw my "family" again. It turns out that I was actually an orphan, groomed to become part of the merging FBI and NSA, assuming a leadership position. All of the questioning had been done by secret agents. They had deemed me ready for the agency, and I had been plucked from their farm system.

Slowly I had climbed through the ranks, becoming the head of the agency in time to guide it through World War III, causing me much stress. Unfortunately, this was an even bigger crisis. And I think my answer to the question had changed in bad ways. I had been an idiot and turned into a liability for the cause. Hopefully there was no trap waiting at MIT.

Will Hartford

Finally, the plane was coasting in for the midair stop. It seemed like an eternity even though it had been only fifteen minutes. I closed my eyes and cautiously flicked out a tendril of consciousness toward Pierre's glowing beacon of activity. "Pierre," I whispered. He snapped to attention both in my mind and in real life. "What?" he snapped at me. "As allies we need to work together and put aside personal differences for the imminent battle," I said calmly. "Fine," was the slow and grudging reply.

I opened my eyes. "Pierre," I said in a normal tone of voice. "Yes, *Dad*?" he replied, forcing the last syllable out from between clenched teeth. "Can you influence emotions?" I asked. "No," he replied. Too quickly, I realized. Was he still hiding something from me that he had discovered? I decided to leave the issue for now. "Then," I said, "you can interfere with the electromagnetic forces that power the implants of the guards and use them to interfere with their emotions."

"Very well," he said. "I will do as *Mr. Roland* says, *Dad*." The emphasis that he placed on the two names in his reply did not escape my keen ears. The relationship was not healed. How deeply and foolishly had I struck with my counterattack? Deep enough to cause a lasting rift? But Pierre and I had too deep of a relationship to fall into that pit. Unless…but no. That wasn't possible. How could Pierre be influenced by Karl when he had no spies to help him?

I shook my head and put myself back into my battle-ready mind-set. What a silly idea I'd had. No way could Karl hack our networks yet. The plane came quite abruptly to a standstill, and I slid forward slightly. "We've arrived at our destination," announced Christian. "Once Pierre takes out the guards, we will uncloak the jet and skydive down to earth." He took in a deep breath. "Pierre, are you ready?"

"Yes sir," replied Pierre. He shut his eyes and focused intently. However, his brow furrowed. I grew worried and dived in to see the source of the problem. Almost instantly I saw what it was: the guards' electromagnetic shields. They were dissipating Pierre's charge as they were intended to do. "Pierre," I whispered, "Python." Pierre would understand. "Gotcha," he replied. Almost immediately the shields went down. Very simple, when you think about it. If you put enough pressure on the circuits and they burst, the shield naturally fails because no one ever builds a fail-safe into the electrical circuits if they burst from an excessive amount of pressure.

One by one, the embers of mental activity disappeared. "Christian," I said, "it's safe to go down." He nodded quickly. Pierre opened his eyes again as the hatch opened. "Get ready," shouted Christian over the sound of air rushing in. Suddenly we dropped quickly and rapidly out of the jet, which would hover above us invisibly until we needed it again.

As the jets of propellant blasted out of the armor, creating thrust to lower us as softly as a feather to the ground, Pierre closed his eyes again. I wondered what he was doing this time. Suddenly the air around him rippled, and he dropped down as a blur. As he hit the ground, he took off as a blur of gray. So he could slow down time. He was automatically heading in the right direction as well. Perhaps he really had lost all sense of free will in the wormhole.

Then the blur of gray came streaking back. Pierre rematerialized as a solid figure. "I forgot about you guys," he said. "Sorry, Dad. The coast looks clear to me. I went to the lock and back, seems all clear to me. No mental activity spotted." Perhaps Pierre was being mentally influenced. But was the time lapse of him running from the lock and back influencing his brain so that he did not feel hostility toward me? Or was he hiding his emotions extremely well?

"Well then," said Christian, struggling to contain his bubbling ecstasy, "we should hurry up and get to the chamber. Pierre, take it away." Pierre nodded. Suddenly there was a ripple around the three of us. I took a step forward, and the world turned into a blur of pixels. "Son," I said, "frankly, I am very proud of you. That you are creating a bubble of time moving at this low velocity should be violating the laws of physics. Either that or the bubble has to be compressed to a subatomic level. I guess we will have to rewrite the rules, since you are breaking them at an unprecedented rate." Pierre beamed. "Thanks, Dad."

We began jogging, watching the world blur around us. Soon we reached the lock chamber. Christian reached out to deactivate the first layer when a hologram with Karl's face on it popped out of nowhere. The bubble of time disappeared, and I jumped backward. "Well, well, well," said that familiar, insinuating voice. "Look who it is. A dead man, a liability, and a loose cannon. Who could have been better for the job?" I froze in shock. No, no, no, no! This could not be happening.

"Oh, poor Will," said Karl in a voice dripping with fake sympathy. "Does he need some help figuring out what the big bad man did to outsmart him? Well, the big man is merciful enough to tell his inferior exactly what he did to thwart the poor fool."

9

CRISIS MANAGEMENT

Karl von Liebnitz

Ha-ha, ha-ha, ha-ha, ha-ha, ha-ha! Tyrannei strikes back with a tremendous blow. Who's inferior now, the man who's supposedly dead or the megamind? That look of shock on the poor sod's face was enough to keep me smiling for a week. Priceless, just priceless. That memory would stick with me for a while. Just unbelievable. Hirschel really deserved a promotion for all of his tireless service. Unfortunately, he was irreplaceable. If I took him out, I would take out my best source of information. Hopefully he won't become envious of others.

I brought my mind back to my projected image being shown to them live. Make this process as slow and tortuous as possible for everyone, I thought. Looking back at the screen, I saw varying degrees of shock on the three faces. Finally,

Hartford spoke. "Karl," he said in an inaudible voice. "How? What—" I shook my head with that same smile on my face. "You're getting old, Hartford. Coming back to life hasn't made you any younger, cheater."

I resisted the urge to burst out in laughter when I saw Pierre's face flicker momentarily with disbelief and then revert to an expressionless look. "Oh, Pierre," I sighed. "For once, the truth has been spoken. Ask your father. If he denies the charges, he is not only a cheater but a liar." The bullet struck home. I read the barely concealed anger in his body language. "Look who's talking," snarled the loose cannon. "The biggest liar ever. Ever heard of a concept called hypocrisy, imbecile?"

Oh, dear me. The boy was really headstrong. How those two managed to contain him, I had no idea. My smile and all traces of happiness vanished in an instant, replaced by an intense, cold, and calculating feeling. "Imbecile, am I, boy?" I crooned softly. Hartford stiffened, knowing that the storm was coming. "Pierre, enough," he snapped. "Do not test Liebnitz beyond the point where we do not get an explanation." The boy did not budge. "No, Dad," replied the boy. "He's a liar; how can we trust his explanation anyway?"

"Pierre, I repeat, do not test Liebnitz beyond his limits," countered Hartford. "There will be worse to come if you do." The boy's reply was already clear. "Yes, hypocrite," he screamed at the screen. "I name you an imbecile!" So much unrestrained potential being shut down so quickly. I sighed in regret. "Let's see who's an imbecile after this," I whispered in cold anger. Hartford closed his eyes.

Quickly I turned the hologram into a mental conduit. Almost instantly, I met Hartford's mental defenses encircling the conduit. I channeled all my anger into a single burst and rammed through Hartford's defenses. He collapsed in agony. I ignored the liability, who had been watching the confrontation through his shock, and concentrated on the boy. My burst of concentrated energy bounced right off the boy's mental defenses.

I reeled backward in surprise. The boy was untrained and a novice. How was his mental strength so disciplined? This should not be happening. Natural ability could not take Pierre so far without any training whatsoever. I guess I would have to do this the hard and painful way. I took down all of my mental safeguards and concentrated my mental energy into a single beam that was atoms thick. I concentrated this beam upon the boy's defenses. They did not even budge a single picometer. No, impossible. No normal mind could withstand my mind's total power concentrated into an atomic beam.

The boy countered my mental onslaught. He swiftly created a wave of energy that shattered my beam, making me scream in mental agony. While my mental energy was shattered and had not recovered completely, he turned his mental counterattack into a hand that slapped my mental circuits, making me scream out loud in pain for the first time in decades. Roland seemed to be thunderstruck by this rare occurrence. The mental hand turned into a fist that surrounded my brain and began slowly squeezing tighter and tighter to the point where my mental circuits were strained to the breaking point.

I began screaming and crying like a baby for the first time since my birth. The boy was so strong and so in control of his power! But I was not becoming a living vegetable if I could help it. That boy was in for it. I could understand how he was fueled by anger that was destroying his reasoning power. If I had foreseen this backlash, I would never have provoked him. "Nein, nein, nein, nein, nein, nein, nein!" I babbled. *"Stopp!"* If I had to replace neurons, I would not stop at anything to get my revenge on that boy.

The fist squeezed ever tighter, and some of my external neurons were beginning to vaporize. I acutely felt the drop in mental strength and reasoning power each time. The boy was acting like a carbon copy of me right now, except with much more unbridled potential. Would he become my successor in world domination?

Suddenly the fist stopped squeezing, but it did not retract. I wondered in my befuddled state what had happened. Certainly nothing I had done. Slowly I recognized a mental shield stopping the onslaught. It was…Hartford's? Was I going mad? What was this? Hartford was protecting me? I also heard the liability screaming at the top of his lungs: "Pierre, stop! Enough! I thought you had a strict moral code! Since when are you fueled by your pure, unbridled anger? Do not become Liebnitz's successor! Do not stoop down to the level of your enemy! Are you a monster as well?!"

Apparently, the boy came to his senses because the fist of mental energy withdrew and with it, Hartford's shield. I stopped screaming and breathed deeply and evenly. I assessed the damage. I had lost neurons everywhere except for my memory and emotional centers. My anger began to fester. I was unsure whether or not I would still give an explanation. I would have to be convinced. This was *not* the way this was supposed to go. I had given way to my baser instincts. Why should I give an explanation from my position of newfound weakness or even negotiate with these thugs?

Will Hartford

What had just happened? Pierre had thrown his emotions out the window. Karl was most certainly mentally damaged by that onslaught, and now he had a larger grudge against Pierre than me. At least that was what I assumed. But Karl still wanted Pierre alive. He wanted me, on the other hand, dead.

I felt bad for Pierre. His tremendous powers came at a tremendous cost. I understood now how conflicted he must feel. He was being deprived of his free will while using his powers, but on the other hand, he wanted to be driven by his moral code. I could only see the two sides of his ego clashing more and more as time went on.

Pierre stood next to me looking like a man resurrected. His face was white, and his mouth hung open in shock as he tried to process the events of the past three minutes. As he fully comprehended the blessing and the curse and his loss of control, he broke down into tears and fell to the floor shaking like a dog. Karl's mind became confused by this apparent conflict of Pierre's personalities. I went over to comfort Pierre and help him resolve the conflict.

Pierre Hartford

I was being torn apart by my two coexisting personalities. Why was I cursed and blessed at the same time? "Morals should always come first!" one of my personalities argued. "Violence and the unleashing of anger and power are the ultimate solution!" my alter personality screamed back. Back and forth it went, argument after argument, splitting my head in two and making me cry.

I saw Dad come over to comfort me. "Please, Dad," I moaned, "leave me alone and let me sort out things on my own. I think Mr. Roland needs your help with...with...Liebnitz." Dad, for once, assented to my request, leaving me a bit surprised but mostly grateful. "All right, son," replied Dad. "But I'm watching you to see what happens while I help Christian."

Dad really had no morals. He cared only about his ambitions and his ultimate goal. I could see the hubris seeping out of him. He was concerned for me because I was his key to winning, and he would be a nonfactor if I went down. I still hated Dad, and I had been forced to show him false love, but for what ultimate goal? That was a question I wanted answered.

Dad joined Mr. Roland in arguing with Liebnitz. I remained curled on the floor, absorbing blows from both sides of my personality. Slowly I slipped out of reality and into the depths of my personality, watching and listening to the battle going on between my two souls, hoping to figure things out:

Moral Personality: The world is a conundrum that can only be solved through peaceful methods. It is so interconnected and diseased that one spark of violence will fan the flames of destruction.

Violent Personality: Ha-ha, tough luck. To rid the world of corruption, one must cut off the source of the disease. That can only be achieved through a bloody and brutal civil war. The leaders must be removed, along with their successors. They will scoff at your futile attempts for peace. They will only go through violent rebellion. What are you, a weak Quaker?

Moral Personality: How dare you call me a Quaker! I am not religious in the slightest, Misguided One. I am, however, a conservative pacifist who believes that violence is the answer for those who are weaklings.

Violent Personality: You dare call me a weakling! Tell me your great moral beliefs then, so I can scoff at them.

Moral Personality: Very well. If you have a chance to let a man live, you let the man live, even if he is your worst enemy. Through persuasive words, you can convince your enemies to join you. Words are the most powerful tools of the intellectual. They shape society and rewrite history, depending on how they are used. We cannot sink to the petty baseness of our greatest enemies, for they are the very beings we do not want to become. The disease will not be cured by installing one tyranny in place of another. War can only be a last resort if all else fails, and that is the only path of salvation. Showing anger toward your enemies will not help you in the slightest. It will only alienate them more from your cause. You think you can still prevail against a united front of barbaric savages? Good luck with that.

Violent Personality: Pshaw! Your arguments are easily brushed aside. Why would you want to become reconciled with your enemy? There is an ideological rift so deep that it can never be healed! If people are neutral, they must choose one side or the other, or they risk being caught in the cross fire. You think the only form of government that violence can create is a tyranny? A democracy can also be created out of violence! What say you to that?

Moral Personality: Well, if you are violent toward neutrals, they will obviously turn against you. Why would they stay on your side? What is the point of that? Of course, you may not be able to convert those who believe the extreme opposite of your viewpoint, but you can persuade those who are neutral to join you. To your second point, have you ever seen a *stable* democratic government created out of a violent morass? All kinds of violently erected governments devolve into despotism or anarchy. Your democracy will be so out of control that you won't be able to keep the people in check unless you counter it with violence! That violence turns your democracy into a tyranny or an oligarchy. Never will you cure the disease with a stable democracy through violence. Through a policy of using violence as a last resort, you bring your moderate enemies onto your side and please all in forming a stable democracy with checks and balances.

Violent Personality: What makes you think that violence to quell rebellion in a democracy will convert my type of government into a tyranny or an oligarchy? To save yourself from the raging mob, you must always use violence. You cannot bring people to your cause with sugared words. Violence as a coercive tool is much more effective than your intellectual weapon of words. If you cannot convince them, just extract information out of them by force and torture. You always have a part of the population on your side.

Moral Personality: The excessive amount of force you are talking about will turn the vast majority of your people against you. This will force you to use even more draconian crackdowns and violence, resulting in a spiraling death cycle of your democracy! Violence does not bring your enemies wholeheartedly onto your side. If they sense your weakness, they will turn against you, or they will work against you in secret. If you are a truly moral person, you will only promise what you know you are able to fulfill in the first place. You would never promise something you cannot fulfill. You see, my method is much more effective than an uneasy peace enforced through violence would ever be. A volatile situation where you use violence will only bring the situation into a higher state of volatility rather than defuse the situation.

Suddenly I realized I was being called through my meditative mist. I wondered how I had become split into two separate but controllable parts. How could they be so independent of my control at the same time? The strength and caliber of their individual arguments and their high intelligence as independent parts of my personality scared me. Hopefully this would not become more of a problem.

"Pierre," shouted Dad and Mr. Roland in unison, "Liebnitz is ready to provide his statement. We would like you to listen to it as well." I stood up unsteadily and looked Liebnitz in the eye. Liebnitz calmly opened his mouth and prepared to begin.

10

HALF OF THE VEIL IS LIFTED

Christian Roland

What had just happened to Pierre? I was positive that he was not fueled by violence and anger but by his strict moral code. Why had he given way to anger and violence? Was his blessing also a curse? Was he losing the free will to use his powers? That was the worst possible way to live. I could feel the split between his moral and violent personalities. I understood his great pain. Oh, that I never had to negotiate again with a snake like Liebnitz.

I would not have a chance to use Pierre for three battles. Oh dear, we would be blown out and destroyed. That was the only negotiating stance Liebnitz had that was remotely reasonable in order for us to hear his statement. His statement had to include secrets that when revealed would cut us dry to the bone and give us extreme pain. Pierre must have made

Liebnitz feel like a weakling to bring on such a humble nego-
tiator. At least we were getting a statement.

Karl von Liebnitz began, "Perhaps I should explain the
Hartford-Liebnitz schism and the rise of Tyrannei to…en-
lighten our audience members who have a lesser understanding of those events.

"I'm sure we all know the embellished story of the schism,
the one where only I look bad and Hartford looks like the
saving grace. I'm sure that almost nothing has been spoken
of Hartford's arrogance and the culture of cheating to win
competitions. Why should one side of the story be kept secret,
while the other side is revealed in its entirety?

"Well, to make a long story short, Hartford and I headed
to our first competition together at ages eleven and six, re-
spectively. Hartford and I were placed on opposite sides of
the draw, and we faced off in the final. Guess what the saving
grace did? He decided to kick a wrench at my bucket of parts
and my final component, spilling them all over the floor. I had
to scramble to find them all, and by then, Hartford had won
the competition. It was ruled an 'accident.'

"I was reprimanded for complaining to the saving grace,
and when I returned the favor at the next competition, I was
berated for sabotaging his project. What hypocrisy and hubris.
The tensions boiled to the point where he had to sabotage my
robot to get into MIT and then had the nerve to berate me for
being 'overly emotional.' I was applying to college early, and I
would have still won the spot! You see how Hartford keeps his

'win at all costs' mentality? That was the end of that. Moving on.

"I wandered through the streets and into an alley, slumping against a wall, and began to cry. Then the best thing that could have happened to me happened. I met a certain Yuri Klatschnikov. He somehow managed to speak in an eloquent fashion, and Tyrannei was formed in the shadow of the Merkel Dumpster.

"I recruited Bartleby and Joubert, and Tyrannei took off. I'm sure you've heard of the Gurov fiasco and the failed assassination, so now let us get to the meat of the story. You wanted an explanation, here you go."

Pierre looked shocked and turned to Will. "Is this true, Dad?" he asked. There was no reply from the stone-faced Will. "Dad, you're no better than Liebnitz if these allegations are true. I should never have trusted you, with your ruthless nature and no morals."

Mr. Roland wisely stayed out of Pierre's barrage launched at Will. In his weakened state, Liebnitz still managed to smile. His introduction was fattening the pigs for slaughter. He continued his statement:

"Before I begin, I must tell you that everything in this statement is true and that I do not expect to be assaulted by your more…radical elements.

"Well, perhaps I should start with the infiltration of the new-look FBI, back in the day. Tyrannei was still in hiding, but we had a strong recruiting network that stretched through Europe and North America. We heard almost immediately when the liability was steered into his new position by the so-called president. As every FBI chief has done, the liability brought in his own staff. We had one specific recruit in mind to put on the liability's staff. He was quite young and passed the tests with flying colors, so he was put on the list of applicants.

"We knew he was a top target for the FBI from the moment he applied. Obviously he got in. Capable, charismatic, and able to follow orders, this man rose through the ranks to become one of the liability's personal bodyguards. He's kept his spying position since the start of World War III. His name is Bradley Hirschel."

Liebnitz let his statement sink in and began to chuckle weakly. Mr. Roland's face turned a dark and ugly shade of purple. "So it was Bradley," he muttered. "Why was he so passive then?" Liebnitz smiled. "Oh, he was only externally passive, my dear liability. During his long tenure, he managed to hack your networks and give us direct surveillance of the FBI bases in which he resided, record your important statements from the shadows, and provide us with some of your technological secrets." Mr. Roland looked stricken, but internally he sighed in relief. The most important secrets were for the most part never revealed to Bradley. "Oh, Liebnitz," muttered Mr. Roland. "You will pay; I guarantee it." He simply smiled. "We'll see about that, liability," was his smooth reply. "Moving on."

Liebnitz continued, "So we had the FBI under our thumb through our conduit of Hirschel. We infiltrated all of the important spy networks. Then, however, Cybor burst onto the scene after World War III had ended. We needed to infiltrate the company quickly, for I saw the caliber of talent Cybor had firsthand. I knew that Cybor had an immense pool of raw potential, so I had the clever idea to send in the dumbest recruit

I could find because I realized that if I sent in my smartest recruit, Cybor's talent pool would recognize him or her instantly. So to beat them at their own game, I sent in my resident imbecile, Kaspar Gurov.

"You all know what Gurov managed to bring upon himself, the fool. I don't think I need to explain *that*. Anyway, *Hartford* here managed to make me play right into his hands. Like a fool, I didn't realize that Gurov's information was unimportant and being spoon-fed to him by Hartford. In return I gave him some partially crucial information that he put on the fast track to give to Hartford.

"At least I wasn't stupid enough to think that Gurov invented the Eye Spy 0.2 when he told me so; I smelled a rat there. I knew Hartford or one of the other scientists was behind *that*. You all know about the attacks, et cetera.

"I celebrated after the successful end of the attacks. Hartford and the board were dead, I had Cybor in my palm, and nothing could stop me now. The juggernaut had risen from the depths of Merkel's Germany and instituted a violent coup, bringing Europe to its knees and creating a solid base of income and resources for Tyrannei to grow even larger. Only the United Kingdom and its powerful ally, the United States, prevented me from expanding ever further, although they could not wipe me off the map. Their wasted money and equipment made me even stronger, allowing me to develop some of the technologies and materials, such as shuritanium, you saw firsthand used by my dear Klatschnikov.

"I'm sure that the goals of Tyrannei are quite clear by now. We are here to cleanse the world of its disease centers and purify the corrupted areas. That means taking over the world, country by country, through violent retaliation. Once we have conquered the entire world, the formation of a new and better government will begin. Anyway, back to shuritanium.

"The story of shuritanium is actually quite interesting. It was serendipitously discovered one day when I was refining the Eye Spy to give to my soldiers. I had salvaged some electric suits from the latest US retreat, back in the days after the Cybor coup, and I was taking them apart to use their electricity generating components in the implants, as the materials the United States used manage to generate a huge amount of electricity in a very small volume.

"I put the disassembled components into a chemical solution so they would interact with the components of the Eye Spy, bringing down costs and using material more efficiently. When all of the components bonded, however, there was a slight chemical reaction that created minute traces of a by-product. When I analyzed these traces, I found a truly amazing material. You all know the specs for shuritanium, so I don't think I need to elaborate. However, someone leaked my discovery to the wider public, as well as the method of making it. That traitor was swiftly destroyed. My rage that day was uncontrollable. Never mind that though, continuing on.

"The material was highly expensive to make, so I only made enough to craft three suits, putting in all of my advanced technology, some of which Klatschnikov did not reveal. Anyway, I had a knockout punch in cases of dire need.

"Hirschel, during his tenure, managed to put some of my own thought scanners onto the surveillance system. This system really helped me to do discreet spying without having to rely on him the whole time. So when Pierre arrived at the FBI base, I knew immediately where he was, even though teleportation is usually untraceable. I also was able to read Pierre's thoughts about his weapon, with its portable wormhole transmitter. Thank you, loose cannon.

"I have not seen the weapon yet because Hartford placed his surface underbug crawler into my system, shutting it down at a crucial moment. However, the liability and Hartford were so loud and brash that Hirschel sent me a recording where you two elaborated upon Pierre's powers. I must thank all of you for your contributions to Tyrannei. It really does help when your enemy can be stupid for you.

"By the way, I told Klatschnikov the coordinates of your base in the Mojave Desert. By now, it is probably wiped off the map. I hacked through your lockdown system by reusing Hartford's surface underbug crawler. It was recognized as part of the system. It managed to shut down the entire power grid, so I hope you said goodbye, for Klatschnikov has an easy target now.

"I built my own fleet of human robots a few years ago. They look and talk like humans, but they are very intelligent and ruthless killers with advanced weaponry and implants. I think I sent, oh, about twenty of them to come to this spot, capture you all, and bring you back to your new home at my base. They have mental blockers to prevent mentalists like the loose cannon from shutting them down, making it nearly impossible to kill them in large swarms.

"You can surrender now and live out your lives in my prisons, or you can die fighting. After all, I only need the loose cannon alive. Well, I think I've revealed enough. Why would I give you details about my secret programs? That would be stupid of me. I guess this is goodbye then, my dear enemies. I will see at least one of you soon enough."

The connection was cut off and the hologram disappeared, leaving Pierre, Will, and Mr. Roland standing there in shock.

Christian Roland

Oh man. Liebnitz delivered some hard punches. Bradley was one of his spies. That piece of information on its own managed to completely ruin my day. The good thing was that Bradley only knew about the external ring, not the internal ring and ancient vaults. Bradley had always been nice and obedient, ready to follow orders and perform any tasks to the best of his ability.

If only Will and I hadn't been so stupid, we would still be keeping some secrets. We had never checked the surveillance system for thought probes. We had been idiots, shouting out Pierre's abilities with our cries of "Eureka!" Some of this was our fault. We could probably escape to live another day though. If Pierre let himself be fueled by his anger, the robots would be down in no time. I hoped dearly, however, that his rage would not completely overtake him again. That was perhaps our only hurdle to winning. Pierre could hold off the robots while I unlocked the chamber. Then we could sprint back to the ship and take off.

I heard the first robots coming with their familiar pattering side step. The first battle had come, and I was about to break the agreement as Liebnitz expected, for he would probably have done that as well in our position. "Pierre," I said calmly, "get ready to take down the robots. Control your violence so we can unlock the chamber and get back to the jet without having any issues from you." Pierre looked back with a steely gaze. "I will do what you ask to the best of my ability, sir," he said. "I am ready for battle." Pierre shrugged and his armor came up and covered his body. The war had finally begun in earnest.

11

A Daring Escape and an Even Bigger Surprise

Pierre Hartford

I think that the moral side of me had won for now in our secret argument. That was good. Hopefully I could keep it that way. What tore me apart was the fact that Dad had in fact helped Liebnitz become the monstrous supervillain that he was now. Dad, unfortunately, had absolutely no morals. It was shocking and saddening. He was like Liebnitz, except that he worked for the FBI. He was utterly ruthless and influenced the world around him because of it.

That was an act that was not driven by any morals; that was just...disgusting, driven by petty selfishness. To top it all off, I found out that Liebnitz knew about the weapon and that Dad was also a liar and irresponsible to boot. Did that mean that he was only using me as a means to a greater end? Was I being manipulated into trusting him, only for him to abandon me on the side of the road in the future? I sincerely hoped not, for then there would be three factions in this already horrible war; we didn't need an interplay among three parties opposing each other.

Finally Liebnitz's aforementioned robots came into sight. If I hadn't known better, I would have said they were human and laid down my weapons right then and there to attempt to negotiate. Thankfully, I knew better. I delved into my consciousness to find my two halves in an uneasy state of peace. Violent, I thought silently, you're going to let Moral run this battle. I don't want any interference from you, or I will make you feel my wrath.

Violent Personality: How are you going to do that, hot-shot? I'm part of your consciousness. I'm the right side of your brain. Lose me, and you lose your creative side. I don't think you want that, buddy.

Moral Personality: I, however, can do something against you, Violent. I can shut you down if you act up. I'm the dominant one here, and you will obey my orders.

Violent Personality: Well, I'll listen to you for now, Moral. But I'm warning you, Master; you'll see that you need me after all soon enough. Just wait till you start the battle.

"Oh no, Violent," I said. "I don't need you to take down these robots. I'm going to prove you wrong." I slipped back into the real world to face the robots. The lead robot turned and faced me. "We are servants of Karl von Liebnitz," it said in a clipped monotone. "We are here to accept your surrender or take only you alive and kill the others. What do you say, boy?" I gave my answer by generating a strong force field that knocked the robots backward. "We fight, Mindless One," I replied calmly. "Prepare to be put out of commission."

And so the first battle of the Liebnitz Offensive began. "Oh, you will regret that, boy," said the robot without changing its facial expression or tone. The robots began to move as clumps and rammed themselves against my mental force field. I flinched internally with each impact. I was really weaker without using anger, but I probably would be strong enough to take them out.

"Boy, just give up. You cannot win against the might of the robot race," said the lead robot again, trying to goad me into making a false move. "Oh no, robot. You're not getting me to snap that easily," I muttered under my breath. I mentally accessed the electrostatic field generator in my armor and programmed it to only target objects with a certain electric charge. I then extended my tendrils to the electric fields surrounding the robots and made them the same charge that the electrostatic field was programmed to hit.

"I think that you've just lost, robots," I said calmly. "Say goodbye." The robot laughed hollowly without any emotion. "We don't go down that easily, boy," was the robot's comeback. As a reply, I switched on my electrostatic field generator and sent an energy surge of seventy thousand gigajoules spiraling out. As if by magic, the bolts of electricity homed in on the robots and surrounded them with electric fields that fizzed and crackled. The fields penetrated their outer armor, and the robots began to behave erratically, jerking their limbs around in a random fashion. Suddenly they partially shattered as their electronic brains shut down and spontaneously combusted. Soon the electric charges faded, leaving twenty fizzing and smoking robots, with random metal scraps scattered around them.

I sighed in relief and relaxed slightly while keeping my force field up, just in case. I looked back at Dad and Mr. Roland. "Sir," I shouted, "I think I put them out of commission." Mr. Roland looked up briefly. "Good job, Pierre," he replied. "We need a few more minutes to unlock the chamber." I smiled in relief. "All right, sir," I replied.

Suddenly, however, I saw something shocking. The robots were beginning to move again. Oh no! How had that field not dispatched them instantly? They shouldn't be getting up again and trying to murder Dad and Mr. Roland. "I...told you... that...we wouldn't...give up...so easily," creaked a robot. "We have...a mission...to accomplish."

Slowly, all of the robots got up and wobbled unsteadily like a pack of drunkards. "Now is when...we get...serious," said a robot. The robots pulled up their hands, which folded into weapons. They began firing laser bursts out of their weapons. The beams hit the force field and dissipated harmlessly, but I felt my strength ebbing. I dug into my reserves and kept the force field up while temporarily creating a bubble around the robots in which time ran at a slower pace, making the robots move more slowly. "Sir," I shouted to Mr. Roland, "we have a very serious problem." He looked up, concerned. "What is it, Pierre?" he asked. "Well, sir," I began, "I shocked the robots with my electrostatic field generator. Unfortunately, the robots don't seem to stay dead. They got back up after they had been partially shattered. I put them in a time dilation bubble, but the effects are temporary and I'm running out of energy."

Mr. Roland brought his brows together. It was, however, my father who answered me. "Pierre," he said, "those robots...

Cybor designed them. Liebnitz stole the design when he took over Cybor. They were designed to withstand strong electrostatic fields meant to take them down, and they have protected mental states, so they can't be influenced to self-destruct. However, Cybor put in kill switches that can't be removed because they contain the brains and motors of the robots. You can't modify the motors without making drastic design modifications to the robots. These modifications would render the robots harmless and make it easy to take them down. So they still have kill switches in them. Mentally flip them. I'll help you hold them back."

I was a bit unsure if the kill switches would work, but I decided to go along since this was the only idea we had. "OK, Dad," I said. "Just help me maintain the force field, and I can trip the kill switches." Dad nodded in agreement. I felt his mental energy combine with mine and keep the robots from penetrating the force field. I first felt my way cautiously into the command center of one of the robots. I saw many components but not a kill switch. I exited the command center and looked quickly around the robot. No kill switch was found. I began to doubt Dad. Then I realized that the kill switch was right in front of me the whole time. The command center structure was shaped like a switch. I flipped the switch into the opposite position and let the time dilation bubble around the robot dissipate.

The robot got up blearily and began to shuffle toward the force field. Then it blew up quite suddenly and scattered its metallic innards over a wide area. I was euphoric. It worked! I felt reenergized and proceeded to blow up the other nineteen robots, watching them scatter their innards across the burned campus. Mr. Roland looked up. "The lock is ready to be opened," he said. Dad and I walked over. Mr. Roland pressed a button on the lock, and it suddenly began to whir and hum.

As each of the water-filled spheres began to open, the water drained and the spheres rotated rapidly as they turned the gears that would release the bolts on the door. Finally the door opened and we walked in. I gasped. Rows of filing cabinets stood lined up against the walls, filling the room. "So many paper files?" I asked, astonished. "Yes, Pierre," said Mr. Roland. "Paper can't be hacked like electronic storage devices. It can only be burned or decay naturally. In the correct conditions, paper can be preserved for a very long time without fear of it being stolen."

Mr. Roland looked around. "If these files get into Liebnitz's hands, we're screwed," he said. "Pierre and Will, can you carry all of these boxes back to the ship to store them?" Dad and I replied in unison, "Of course we can." I lifted up most of the boxes and let Dad take the rest. "Oh yes," added Mr. Roland, "make sure you can easily transport the files that we're going to have in storage in the Turbojet quickly and efficiently. We're going to be changing vehicles at some point during our return trip to a different base." I wondered what kind of stealth ship Mr. Roland had that could fit all of these files and give us ample room to move around and pilot the ship. "All right, sir," I said.

I quickly placed the boxes and us into a time dilation bubble and made time slow down around us. We rapidly moved back to the ship. We shot up into the belly of the Turbojet, propelled by our jet packs. We were just in time, coincidentally, as all of the guards at MIT happened to wake up. However, they could not prevent us from taking off safely, and we left them behind to shake their weapons at us.

Soon, however, we had something else to worry about. "Christian," said Dad, who was piloting the Turbojet, "we have some incoming scout ships that are getting ready to aim and fire. Permission to engage in evasive maneuvers and take them out?" Mr. Roland considered quickly. "Permission granted," he replied. "Try not to overdo it though." Dad did not reply. Instead he tilted the nose of the ship down so quickly that I left my innards far behind, high up in the air.

Dad suddenly pulled the nose up and sent us spiraling into a loop-the-loop. Through the windows I could see some missiles missing us by inches. There really must be some good shooters in those scout ships, I thought. Dad returned fire. Behind us I heard some muffled booms, which I took to signify that the ships had been destroyed.

We sat back and relaxed. I felt reassured that we were out of range. However painful the loss of the FBI base might be, I knew we were probably headed somewhere even safer, out of the reach of Agent Hirschel. I had won this round against Violent, but I realized that Moral would have to cede some control if I were to take down tougher enemies and not exhaust myself.

Just then an incoming message showed up on the dashboard. The name displayed was Karl von Liebnitz. Oh dear. What was happening now? The Turbojet jerked erratically, and Dad's knuckles whitened on the controls. He opened the message. Liebnitz's voice filled the room.

"I see that you three managed to escape from some of Hartford's old technology and took down my scout ships as well. I congratulate you on securing a bit of your freedom for a while longer. However, I am withdrawing my offer of surrender. You are now wanted dead no matter what, except for dear Pierre. You broke the terms of our agreement by having Pierre take down my robots. I think that counts as a battle. The terms of the agreement stated that Pierre would be kept out of three battles. So the offer of surrender has been withdrawn.

"Oh yes, this is a special message for the liability. I believe I forgot to mention this before. If you do go into even more secluded hiding, I have something that may coerce you to change your decision. You see, you did not protect potential hostages very well. I took them into my custody. Here is your proof, dear liability."

Calls of "Dad?" could be heard on the message. Mr. Roland turned white and looked as if he tried not to lose his temper. Liebnitz continued, "You see, if you do decide to go into hiding with your friends, Roland, I have your wife and children. One of them will die every week until you decide to come out of hiding and be executed. Your choice. That is my ultimatum, liability. Family or country? I do think you would answer that question differently now, don't you think? Well, I'll give you twenty-four hours to come to a decision. Goodbye."

The connection was broken. I felt pity for Mr. Roland flow into my heart. What a dilemma for him. I had a feeling that we were going to launch a rescue operation instead of going into hiding. I hoped not, since that would probably be a dumb idea, but sometimes heart overrules head. I turned toward Mr. Roland to see him sobbing, considering the fate of his loved ones.

12

THE ROLAND DILEMMA

Christian Roland

Internally, I was beating myself up. Why and how could I have forgotten my family and let Liebnitz take my wife and children? Things like this didn't just slip my mind. Of that, at least, I was still sure. That led me to a more disturbing question: Why had I decided to even start a family in the first place? People in high-level government positions shouldn't have families; it was too easy for terrorists to grab hostages and create a different answer to that all-important question we agents had to answer from our hearts to gain admission to the government.

From the moment that I had married my dear wife, I knew that my answer to that question had changed. That could have gotten me fired from my prestigious FBI position. However, I was too entrenched in my leadership role. The answer to that question showed the government a lot about your true personality and if you were a viable candidate to become a federal employee.

That all-important question was: What would you do if you held the fate of the world and humanity in your hands? Would you let humanity live, although the world was corrupt and diseased, or let the world die, along with the majority of humanity? I had given the correct answer, saying that I would not save the world. For humanity to start over and not fall into the same traps as its ancestors would be a blessing.

However, I had grown too attached to my family. I wanted to save my loved ones but didn't have enough power to do so if Earth was destroyed. And here is where my perhaps fatal flaw came into play. I could not let go of any of the people I cared for and would put them before anything else in my life. That meant that I wouldn't be able to destroy Earth if it came down to that. I should have retired instead of staying in power and increasing the fragility of the government. Why did they leave sentimental old men in place to run the government?

This flaw meant that I wanted to launch a rescue operation right here and now, although my rational, reasoning mind knew that was an act of sheer stupidity. I promised myself to hold my impulsive mind in check until we reached the base and could plan a rescue mission.

Through great effort and a lot of pain, I managed to force some particularly painful words out of my mouth: "Continue on to Liebnit...no, I mean base, our current destination, remember we are switching vehicles to mount a res...no, to throw Liebnitz off our trail." I sank down into my seat, completely drained by the effort it had taken to force the words out of my mouth. It was as if my mind tried to make me sabotage our mission, although that was a ridiculous notion. Pierre looked at me with concern. "Please stop, I don't want to earn your pity as if I were some petty little beggar," I prayed to myself.

Pierre looked away and gave me a thumbs-up. "Very well," came his voice from inside my head. "Let us talk this way, inside of your mind, away from Dad's influence. I'm not blind. I can see the ropes that bind you to him, so I've decided that we need to have a private conversation without Dad's interference." I nodded mentally. "OK then," I thought back at Pierre's presence in my mind.

The mental conversation

Pierre: Mr. Roland, sir. I'm very sorry about your family being taken hostage, but I'm sure that some see your decision to start a family as foolish. If I may ask without being offensive, sir, could I please hear the whole story so I can give you some sound advice?

Christian: Pierre, my story…well, it's very long, emotional, and complicated. A kidnapped child groomed for power but struck down by petty love and foolishness. What a way for leaders to fall from the very zenith of their careers into the depths of darkness. I think, though, that your advice will be quite helpful to me, Pierre. After all, we both suffer from split-brain personality syndrome. I also have two halves of my brain trying to assert dominance, although I have no mental powers like you. First, I will tell you my story.

I remember being part of a happy and stable family. I was

not spoiled but worked hard for every possession I owned. I was proud and happy. The strange thing about my childhood, however, was that unusual people would always visit me and ask me a long series of questions that I grew accustomed to. They bored me half to death with their droning voices and strange behavior. One day a woman came to interrogate me. I was asked the same questions, but then she suddenly asked me a different and fateful question.

Pierre: Can you give me an example of a few boring questions, sir?

Christian: Yes, I can. All right, listen up. Here's an example: If I walked away from you, what would you do? My reply: I would leave you alone and let you gather your feelings and regain your composure. Another example: How much are you willing to sacrifice for the needs of the United States? My reply: I would give up everything if it helped my country. As for that fateful question: If you held the fate of the world in your hands, would you let it, and by extension humanity, live even though humanity is diseased and corrupt, or would you let the world die and by extension most of humanity? I said that I would let the world die so we could start anew.

Pierre: That is the correct answer, sir. I would have given the same one. An interesting question to use as an entrance exam, but I'm not going to argue. They did pick you as their next FBI chief, and they made an excellent choice. I don't think that they wanted that answer though, since it would doom them if their fate did fall into your hands, as all government agencies these days are corrupt. Continue on.

Christian: That is an interesting way to look at that question, Pierre, although I think the government officials suspect they will find a way to save themselves from my destructive decision. They also demand utmost loyalty, so they might find a way to subtly change my mind through careful persuasion. I have given the government nothing but my utmost loyalty, and I expect to keep it that way. I've had the viewpoint that the government is corrupt virtually wiped out of my mind, so I'm afraid that on that point we cannot agree, Pierre.

Moving on, I was admitted to the FBI the day after the woman had come. I never saw any of my interrogators ever again. I realized that my admission to the FBI might not have been completely by chance. I learned that my "family" had been handpicked to care for me and that I was in fact an orphan. That meant that I had never had a real family since the one I had, had done everything for me only because of orders from the FBI. The fact that I was just another ripe apple plucked from a tree by the FBI made me bitter. It has never left my heart, although it has been buried very deep.

I quickly rose through the FBI ranks, leading counterespionage teams by the time I was eighteen, back in 2014. My superiors were so impressed with me that I was quickly nominated to be first a major general, then a commander of a continental division of agents, and finally commander in chief of the FBI, all by the age of twenty-two. I accepted, becoming the youngest FBI director ever. Soon after I had assumed leadership, the FBI merged with the NSA to adopt its new name.

Soon after that, World War III began, and I had to whip the new FBI into shape and make sure it didn't fall apart during our toughest fight yet. Those were some of my darkest days, with the agency nearly shutting down at points. Those days brought on lots of stress that I only managed to get under control much later, but it was too late. I was already diagnosed with depression, bipolar disorder, and schizophrenia. It's been a hard battle, but I've managed to survive.

I was tough and battled through adversity. Once the war ended, I got proper treatment, but those demons still haunt my head at times. World War III was grueling, but at least the war was for the most part an offensive slugfest, which meant that more lives potentially could have been lost. Eventually the Allies overpowered the Middle East and the Pacific Rim, resulting in a tenuous peace and a second era of colonialization and empire building that I strongly disagreed with, fearing something like Tyrannei would spring up from that boiling pot. My advice, however, was not heeded by the hot air balloon that was our president.

From there, everything went down. Although peace seemed to reign supreme and everything seemed calm, underneath the surface violent sentiments were boiling over into violent underground movements, the foremost of which was Tyrannei. This exacerbated the problems of our ailing world. The worst part: we were dangerously close to ending our world anyway. Carbon emissions were at an all-time high, and we were metric tons away from crossing the threshold of two degrees Celsius.

Then the government did its savior act by introducing Cybor and your father. Their technologies slashed the carbon emissions into nothingness. The world was saved from global warming, but we are and always have been humanity's greatest enemy. Our propensity for killing off our own kind has been shockingly high. That is the only reason that I even have a job. It's maddeningly ridiculous and shocking.

My job became increasingly stressful as the buildup of

underground violence increased. Then Tyrannei burst onto the scene, conquering Germany and its affiliate satellite states. We threw a boatload of money at Tyrannei. Nothing happened. We basically donated its entire start-up fund, which enabled it to conduct advanced research. That is why I fear this war, along with my hostage crisis. I fear that this will be World War IV after all the red tape will have been unraveled. This is my story, Pierre, and I need some advice.

Pierre: Under no circumstances can you let your emotional center overtake you, or we will be forced into a stupid situation. We must get into your secret base. We can then consider a rescue operation when it also benefits us from the standpoint of the greater war. We need to force Liebnitz's hand but not in an exclusive rescue mission. You also cannot let your governmental loyalty override you analytical brain. We may need to disobey government orders and break off from the rest of the corrupt system in order to smash it up in a better fashion.

The way to shut down your mind is to erect a virtual barrier around your emotional center and keep your mind off emotional subjects to the best of your ability. This is the only advice that I can give you, sir. If this fails, I have no idea what I'm supposed to do.

Christian: I will follow your advice to the best of my ability, Pierre. I am not sure that I would be willing to split the FBI and its entire force into offshoots fighting against the government because that might cause some unrest within the ranks. However, I see the point of your advice. I do not know if I have the ability to erect a barrier strong enough to keep my mind off the things that are dear to my heart, but I will also try to do that to the best of my ability. Anyway, I think we've reached the vehicle switch point.

Pierre and Mr. Roland ended their mental conversation and returned to the real world. Will landed the Turbojet, and the three companions stepped onto the ground. A decision had been made, and the journey would continue.

13

NEW HORIZONS

Will Hartford

I had noticed the mental activity inside Christian's head and assumed that Pierre was having a mental talk in the only way he could with a person like Christian who did not possess mental abilities. I suddenly came to a realization that Pierre was not a baby, that he was much more mature than I ever could be, with my backstabbing ways and petty Pyrrhic victories. I should not treat him like a complete novice all the time. I had to let him unleash his potential and deal with his demons in his own fashion and in his own time. Then I could pick up the pieces because I was pretty sure that Pierre would go completely out of control and at some point destroy the corruptness I hated. Of course he wouldn't destroy me, his father.

If Pierre was very mature, he would have given Christian very sound advice that we would not under any circumstances head into a foolish and suicidal rescue mission for his family unless we also had some ulterior motives to do so. Without uttering a single word, I knew that Christian wanted me to stay the course.

As the three of us stepped onto the ground, Pierre and I opened the cargo bay and hauled the boxes down safely to be transferred to the cargo bay of our next vehicle. At least that was what I had been thinking until I saw the vehicle. It was a rusting Osprey series jet from the early 2000s that looked more like a museum piece than an aircraft that would be able to transport three people and a bunch of heavy boxes. "Christian," I asked calmly, "are you sure that we've landed at the right place?" I began to have seeds of doubt in my mind.

"Yes," replied Christian, "we've definitely landed at the right place." OK, Karl must be mentally controlling Christian through Bradley's machinations. "You mean," I began, "that we're supposed to fly in that hunk of junk and not expect it to fall apart at the lightest touch? Christian, you have to consider that our cargo is quite heavy and that we are three people. I don't think that aircraft will be able to safely transport us."

"Oh, don't worry, Will," replied Christian. "I have some sound reasoning as to why we are switching from the Turbojet to the Osprey. First, this is not a museum relic but a working model that I recently piloted with double the cargo of what we have here. It was completely safe, and not a single thing went wrong. The Osprey is in prime flying condition for its age, which means that we are completely safe flying in it.

"Second, I am almost certain that Liebnitz can track us through the Turbojet with some homing beacons that he probably got Bradley to attach. However, Bradley and his friends have never even touched this Osprey, and I highly doubt that Liebnitz would have put homing beacons on this aircraft anyway. Third, although the Osprey is slower, it also is smaller than the Turbojet and has better handling, allowing for more precise maneuverability. We will need every single bit of maneuverability to safely land the ship inside the hangar we are flying to. That is my bit of sound reasoning for you, Will."

I must admit, Christian's reasoning was sound and provided quite a bit of reassurance for me, but just to make sure, I scanned every one of Christian's neurons and brain regions. One could never be too careful with Karl and his spies lurking around every corner. My scan came up clean. I made a mental image of the inside of the Osprey and checked every nook and cranny of the ship. That scan came up clean as well.

"Well, Christian," I said, "your reasoning has convinced me. I will go with you." However, I saw that Pierre's brow was furrowed. "We better leave now," said Pierre. "Liebnitz's drones are already coming. They're probably zeroing in on the homing beacon because we've stopped." With one burst of strength, Pierre and I quickly moved the boxes into the cargo bay of the Osprey. Christian pulled out a control with a miniaturized radar dish on top. "Christian," I began, "what—"

Christian pressed a button on the control. The radar dish began to pulse, sending out a sonic laser beam. It impacted a patch of sand on the ground in front of the Turbojet. Suddenly the ground slid open and the Turbojet slowly floated down into an apparently hidden hangar. Christian turned and looked at me. "This increases the likelihood that we, in Liebnitz's mind, reached our destination, Will," he said. "Liebnitz will think we're in a secret base because this is an unmarked, unfinished hangar that he doesn't know about. We're ready to go now."

The three of us scampered onto the Osprey, and I jumped to the controls. We slowly started moving. I slammed the throttle forward, and the Osprey bucked like a wild horse and shot forward like a rocket. "You didn't tell me, Christian," I panted, "that you modified the jet to fly at supersonic speeds." I was impressed. Christian must have been preparing for this inevitability that was called World War IV for many years. Was this foresight…or paranoia? The unfinished hangar, the miniaturized radar dish, the remodeling of the Osprey—he must have correctly predicted Pierre's emergence as a game changer and his own liabilities years in advance, or his diseases had gotten the better of him. But what would occur if this happened during the war to come?

"I didn't tell you about a lot of things that I've prepared for World War IV. For one and a half decades now, I have been afraid that this would happen," said Christian. "There's a lot that I had to do to prepare for a crisis like this, Will. It took quite an amount of effort and patience to accomplish. I consider myself lucky to have had as much time as I did in the end to prepare for this defensive slugfest. Let's hope that everything works out now."

I wondered why Christian would not teleport us to wherever we needed to go. Probably his careful nature was warning him not to do so because teleportation is sometimes traceable, even with the latest technology. Well, there was a lot of stuff I hadn't told Christian either. I guess we would need to sit down and have a nice, long conversation, along with Pierre. I reached over to turn on the cloaking systems and prime the weapons in case we were being followed.

"No, Dad, don't do what I know you're about to do!" yelped Pierre. I jumped, and my hands drew away from the cloaking and weapons controls. "Why, Pierre?" I asked. Now I was confused. There wasn't a homing beacon, right? Pierre prepared to explain himself. "There's a homing beacon that's currently deactivated. If we turn on the cloaking devices or prime the weapons, it switches on. So we're going to have to rely on speed and evasive maneuvers if it comes to that. The reason we even have a homing beacon is that this Osprey is an old German model used in World War III. The Germans put homing beacons on their ships with those connect switches that were so novel back then. Liebnitz got hold of the entire network of those beacons, so he can see us if we turn on the cloaking devices or prime the weapons."

I was shocked. How had I not discovered the homing beacon, even if it was deactivated? Either Pierre was exponentially more powerful than I, or I had made a mistake. Pierre seemingly picked up my thinking because he suddenly said, "Dad, you forgot to scan the outer hull and armor of the Osprey." I internally smacked myself for becoming so lax. How could I forget to scan the skin…Oh God, I must really be getting old.

"If you want, Dad, I can take over the controls from you," Pierre said helpfully. "I had taken Aerial Maneuvering III at MIT before…it got destroyed." I gratefully accepted his offer, and Pierre went to pilot the Osprey. I slid down into a seat next to Christian.

"Oh, Christian," I sighed, "I'm really getting old. Forgetting to scan the hull of the ship for homing beacons—oh, that was a rookie mistake." Christian looked back at me with a strange expression. "Honestly, Will, it's probably more my fault than yours. I should have scanned the ship when I was first rebuilding it. I would have picked up the signal instantly."

"Since you're a liability because of your hostage crisis and I'm getting too old, I guess it's time that we pass the torch into Pierre's hands and let him assume leadership, while we take backstage roles," I replied. Christian gave me a sidelong glance. "Will, we'll still have to have partial leadership responsibilities. Hasn't Pierre told you this already? Your son has split-brain personality syndrome."

I sat back, shocked to the extreme. Pierre? Split-brain personality syndrome? But how? Pierre had been perfectly healthy just a few days ago at MIT. The answer came crashing down on me with the force of a giant sledgehammer: the wormhole. So much was caused by just that one trip. But that meant his powers were connected to his violent side. Oh, dear God, save us from utter destruction. Maybe this would not be as easy for us as I thought it would be.

"Christian," I began slowly, "Pierre has split-brain personality syndrome?" Christian looked back at me. "Yes, Will," he replied. "He offered me some advice on combating it just now in our mental conversation." I sank back into my seat, feeling utterly defeated. We had no capable leaders. A threesome consisting of a liability, an old man who should be dead, and a loose cannon had to lead our organization in the face of the mighty Tyrannei and its affiliates. We would definitely have to figure something out. The Osprey continued along to its destination, leaving all three of us battling with our minds.

Soon after Christian, Will, and Pierre had departed in the Osprey, the first of Liebnitz's drones arrived at the site of the homing beacon implanted in the Turbojet. The drones blasted the sand in a fifty-foot radius around the location, dropping several heat-seeking missiles straight into the sand, but the missiles all exploded on the surface.

The drones, however, were undeterred in their attempt to find the Turbojet. They unleashed a barrage of cutting laser beams at the sand, switching tactics and trying to cut away the apparent metal lying between them and the Turbojet. But these laser beams, too, were met with failure.

Watching through the cameras, Liebnitz was confused. He was even more confused than usual because he was disobeying his own guidelines and stressing his brain too much after artificial neural growth surgery. He was having trouble thinking straight in the usual manner because his brain still had to catch up with what his limbs were doing on the outside.

Liebnitz was conscious enough to realize that perhaps a different class of lasers was needed to deactivate the lock rather than an attempt to destroy the reinforced hangar ceiling through brute force, wasting expensive ammunition and energy. He twitched a control and the drones unsheathed their sonic radar dishes. He pressed another button. The drones generated pulsed sonic laser beams, sweeping over the sands.

This time his weapons paid off. There was a grinding sound and the ground began to retract, blowing sand and dust into the air. Slowly but surely a large room with bright floodlights was revealed. Right below the entrance stood the prize that Liebnitz had searched for: the Turbojet. He jubilantly waved his arms in celebration, for he was sure that he had thwarted the FBI once again. Little did he know that he had been duped by the oldest trick in the book.

14

DISCOVERY OF THE INNER SANCTUM

Karl von Liebnitz, at the time of the end of chapter 10

The hologram connection fizzled out. My statement was over. On purpose, I had made sure not to tell Roland my dirty little secret: that I had taken his wife and children hostage. It was the one thing that could cut him dry to the bone and make him an optimal turncoat. I smiled, but almost immediately I felt extreme pain course through my skin as if I were being lowered into an acid bath.

How did Pierre control this power? That was a very interesting conundrum. If I could rewire someone's brain so every muscle movement was connected to the part of the brain regulating pain, I would drive myself insane in the process by burning up all of my energy.

I tried to send orders through my neural pod for the surgeons to cart me to the operating room for artificial neural growth surgery, but my pod had shorted out. As quickly as I could, I whipped my hand around and slammed down on the emergency hospitalization button. I screamed and writhed on the floor from the pain received in the ensuing seconds.

"*Du hast gerufen*, Meister?" asked Heinz, my head surgeon, through the intercom. "Ja, ja, ja, ja!" I screamed through the intercom. "*Komm schnell!*" The connection cut off, and I felt as if my head had been split in half.

The door to my office slid open. Heinz burst in with his best medical staff. "Meister," he said, "I am here. I will transport you to the operating room, and then you can tell me what happened to you and what type of surgery you need."

With a snap of his fingers, Heinz activated a holostretcher. Light beams encircled me in a lightweight tube. Pulling a control out of his pocket, Heinz deftly maneuvered the stretcher through the door and into the nearby operating room. I was placed on the bed. Almost instantly, thin tubes snaked into my arms to induce anesthesia. I moved my hand and only felt a small twinge of pain.

"Heinz," I said rapidly, "artificial neural growth surgery. Got attacked mentally, and many neurons were electrified in a squeezing assault. Need them regrown now. Must get back to action quickly." Heinz nodded. "I'm going to put you under and let you get into a meditative state before waking you up. I would suggest that you take this time to do some deep thinking. This is a once-in-a-lifetime opportunity."

I nodded, feeling the pain coming back and then receding completely as I blanked out to the sound of Heinz using a laser drill to cut open my skull.

Meditative state

I woke up to the sensation of weightlessness, floating in a thoughtless void, completely empty and tranquil. I felt at peace with myself, a feeling I had never had before. I relaxed and began to contemplate my next steps in countering that annoying threesome. I did have that prerecorded message for the liability to listen to. I knew for sure that listening to the message would shake him up quite a bit and that he could be driven off the deep end by it. However, I could not rely on that possibility by itself. I dealt not in probabilities but in certainties.

I was positive that Hartford and his son would hold the liability in check, so that meant I would weaken him, but I could not neutralize him in one fell swoop. There was also the chance that Pierre's power would consume him and that he would turn against everything and do the job for me. I would probably not be exempt from that burst of raging power, and neither would the earth, leaving me lifeless and bereft of an empire to rule over.

Hartford was a middle-aged man at this stage, but so was I. He could make a slipup and let me win, or I could slip up and increase the probability of Hartford humiliating me once again. The vehemence I put into that thought caused the void to ripple outward and ring like a gong. Slowly the peace that I had created was shattering. At least I could follow their movements because of a simple homing beacon that Hirschel had placed into their vehicle. After all, there was no need for something convoluted and complicated when the problem could be answered using a simple solution.

I knew they would likely go to an off-the-grid base that I wouldn't know about because Hirschel had never been to those locations, so I had also sent out scout ships to track their Turbojet once it took off. I knew there was no chance that the robots would actually defeat them and prevent them from accomplishing their goal.

I had also just explicitly told the three that I only wanted Pierre alive. But did that mean I was losing the edge to my ruthlessness? Normally I would kill Pierre because of what he had done to me and the fact that I could not control him through my usual methods. So why was I keeping him? Did I actually think that I could provide a compelling argument for him to switch sides? I did not operate this way.

Had I been hit that hard by his mental onslaught that my personality was changing, something that could not be corrected by the surgery? Was I becoming a soft piece of flabby rubber? No! That could not happen! Tyrannei had to prevail, and the world had to be cleansed of— Even in my mind, I was choking on the word "disease." No! This was impossible! One's consciousness was independent from one's brain. Or that was the current scientific consensus.

This could not be happening. Not to me. If I was going soft, I would be eaten by the very scumbags I had recruited. Klatschnikov, Joubert, and Bartleby all vied for the top spot... especially Bartleby. I was positive that I must hide this weakness very carefully.

Anyway, what had I been thinking of before going off on this tangent? Ah yes, the tracking of the Turbojet and the deployment of the scout ships. Now, the scout ships had an enormous range of firepower and weaponry to play with, and the drones that I had deployed should be able to uncloak any concealed secret base they would come across.

Hopefully I was not losing my touch. If I was, I would never have the strength of will or sheer ability to ever realize my ultimate dream. But if the plans I had already instituted did their job correctly, I would not need to utilize my abilities in the future.

But maybe I wouldn't need to be so mercilessly ruthless after all. If I could use my powers without having to be the ruthless, soulless sadist I was, that would be excellent. If I could rule through compassion and not an iron fist, would I not expend less power? That was, after all, the point of being a ruler. Rulers have to be strong and also be able to rule with a benevolent hand. How else can you sympathize with the people you rule?

Nein! I screamed in my brain, making the entire void vibrate from the force of my voice. The void began to ripple in an unstable fashion. I must rule with an iron fist! I cannot let my weak side overtake me! Nein! The void began to dissolve, with Heinz looking over me.

I woke up screaming my thoughts out for the world to hear. My rant continued, undeterred by the change of venue. Heinz instantly looked concerned and strained to make himself heard over my tempestuous rant. "Meister, nein, nein! Calm down or we will not be able to successfully rehabilitate your brain!"

Heinz's entreaties, however, were useless. Although I heard them, I could not stop. I kept on screaming, feeling as if I were going to shatter into pieces like a lightbulb. Heinz burst into a mountain of sobs, and with his hands quivering like collapsing buildings during a strong earthquake, he cried, "Forgive me, Meister."

Heinz's hand sneaked around me and hit a lever. As he fell into a crying heap on the floor, I felt a pure dosage of unfettered, turbocharged electricity surge through me and head for my brain. My screams became even louder, and then the electricity rendered me unconscious again.

When I finally woke up, I was calm and composed. I thought about what I had been thinking before and was ecstatic to find that there was no resistance to my thought process. I was whole once again.

Heinz looked at me, quivering. "Forgive me, Meister!" he cried out. "It was all for your own good. I swear it on the Holy Spirit, cross my heart!" I could see the fervor Heinz was working himself into because of fear of my punishment, and I decided to calm him down. "You are forgiven, Heinz," I replied calmly. "I felt as bad as you did in that moment. Now, as for the start of the accelerated rehabilitation process."

Heinz looked as if he had just been inflated back to his original size. His smile stretched from one side of his face to the other, and he could barely resist skipping around my stretcher to the rehabilitation equipment. "Yes," he said, struggling to contain his relief, "the rehabilitation process. I have the slides right here and the helmet. You understand this process, ja? Through the helmet, all of your memories will be projected, as well as the basic concepts and advanced principles that go along with them. This should theoretically bring back your mental state to approximately what it had been before you were attacked."

"I understand, Heinz," I replied. "Begin the rehabilitation process." I slipped on the metal helmet, and Heinz pressed one or two buttons on a control panel. The helmet tightened around my skull and I was once again in a void, one where I found peace. The process was beginning, and the memories of my early childhood were now projected on the screen: "Karl, age two, learning the difference between good and bad," read the text. I was sucked back into my early childhood…

15

THE REALIZATION OF YOUTH
AND MISTAKES LONG PAST

Karl von Liebnitz's memories

I was a quirky two-year-old. I knew that somehow I was different from other children my age. None of the other children I knew were able to talk coherently yet, or read books. I was proud of myself for being so much smarter than all the other baby numskulls.

Although I was very strange and much smarter than the other babies, I was in the worst parental situation possible. My mother wanted to murder my father for being so abusive, but she did not have the strength or resources for murder or even a divorce, so she remained in her deplorable situation with no way out. My mother was always kind to me and made me feel better at times when I needed it.

My father, on the other hand, was a nasty piece of work.

Whereas my mother came from a rich and cultivated background, my father grew up living on the streets as part of a violent street gang. He was an alcoholic and a drug addict who never completely got over his problems. According to my father's thinking, violence was the answer whenever he got angry. My mother, on the other hand, could always reason her way out of tough situations.

Eventually my father's affiliations with violent crime led to his incarceration in one of the secret Merkel asylums, where he was whacked into shape to rejoin society as a law-abiding citizen. My father kept his temper and emotions in check for a time. Then he met my mother. To this day, I still do not understand what my mother saw in him. Improbably, the couple fell in love and quickly got married. Soon after, I was born.

I was the reason that a great chasm opened up between my parents. There were long arguments about how I should be raised. My father wanted me to toughen up and, because of my laziness, used daily beatings to turn me into a fighter, not a wimp. My mother, however, wanted to cultivate my intelligence and teach me the art of subtle persuasion. This standoff led to innumerable arguments between my parents, all because of me. As both of my parents were typical Merkelian Germans, they decided to be stubborn dunderheads and didn't back away from their positions.

Things came to a head one day when I was two. My father came home while I was having my afternoon snack, which my mother had just prepared for me. Just as my father came in, I dropped my spoon and spilled some food. The spoon was a very heavy iron utensil, which my father forced me to use to build up my strength. Because it was so heavy and there was so much food on the spoon when I dropped it, it hit the floor so hard that the food splattered all over the walls and the tablecloth.

My father turned around slowly, his eyes burning with rage. At this early age, I did not know the difference between good and bad yet. I did not understand why my parents talked so loudly, but I thought it must be normal. So I did the worst thing I could have possibly done while my father was angry. I thought the food splattering on the walls was funny, and I began to laugh.

"Karl," growled my father. "Why do you laugh? This is not funny! You have made our house dirty. Now I must make you dirty, you fool." I thought that Father was joking, so I started to laugh even harder, making the room even dirtier because bits of food were flying out of my mouth. "*Karl!*" screamed my father. "*Enough!* You will stop and clean up your dirty mess, foolish son! I should never have taken you into this household! You have no strength! It is all that stupid woman's fault for teaching you the persuasive ways!"

I stopped laughing as my father finished his tirade. However, he was not done with me. First, he picked me up and put me in my crib, which for some inexplicable reason had been moved into the kitchen. "You. Are. Not. My. Son. Anymore!" he screamed at me. Then he picked up a heavy metal chair and hurled it at my crib. Somehow the chair hurtled by right above my crib but did not hit it, missing by about a quarter of an inch. The chair slammed into the wall and got stuck, raining chunks of plaster and aluminum down on my crib. I began to have a new feeling—fright—so I began crying.

More objects hurtled past my crib. My father began picking up the glass objects from the table and throwing them at me. They shattered against the wall, and the sharp glass shards rained down around me. My mother came out of the living room. "Hans, what is all this commo—" began my mother. Then she saw what my father had already done and how I was curled up into a small, quivering, sobbing ball.

"Hans!" shouted my mother. "*Genug! Er ist noch ein kleines Kind!*" My father, however, was not inclined to listen to my mother. "*Aus dem Weg!*" he shouted. My mother did not budge. "Hans, this is your son, and you will not treat him this way," she said. "Otherwise he will grow up to be an even bigger fool than you are, and you are the biggest fool I know." My father stiffened and stopped before throwing another glass figurine at me.

Suddenly I realized that my mother was doing something "good" so that my "bad" father would stop the "bad" action of throwing objects at me and making me feel "bad." The difference between good and bad dawned on me immediately. It would make this "bad" situation and my "good" mother all the stronger in my memory, creating psychological scars that would never heal properly.

Just as quickly, I realized that my mother was acting as a sacrifice in order to protect me. "Nein!" I screamed loudly. "*Mach es nicht, Mutti!*" However, both of my parents disregarded my plea for peace. My father looked as if he were bubbling in rage. "You will pay for that insult, woman," he growled. With the fist that was not crushing the glass figurine, he hit my mother so hard in the face that she flew across the room and through the wall, collapsing part it. I screamed in fear. My father came toward me.

"Now, as for you, son," he said, "it is time that you learn how to respect your elders. I think that you need a lesson in obedience, just like your mother." I quivered in fear. If my father had not been interrupted at that moment, I don't know what he would have done to me. As he advanced toward me, the door behind him opened. It was our kind neighbor who brought us food when my father was not home.

He stood there, almost fainting in shock. My father turned around slowly. "Ulrich," he said cautiously, forcing a smile onto his face, "how nice to see you." Ulrich, however, did not smile back. "This is domestic abuse, Hans," he said in a chilling voice. "This will be your second stint in the asylum, so you're going to be there for life." My father's face paled instantly, and I saw him scared for the first time in my life. He seemed to grow paler and paler until he looked like a skeleton, and I could almost see him reliving his first stint in the asylum. "Nein, nein, nein," he muttered. Grasping for straws, he pulled a thick wad of cash out of his pocket, more money than I had ever seen before.

"You saw nothing," said my father. Ulrich, however, refused the money. "I don't take bribes, you scumbag," he replied coldly. "You don't deserve to be free for another day. I'm calling the police. Enjoy the rest of your life in the asylum." My father fainted from fear and fell onto the floor with a dull thump. I was surprised. My father could have the same feelings about a place that I could have about him? I thought that it was physically impossible for my father to be scared.

Ulrich called the police. Two police officers came and took my father into custody. I only saw him once after that, and that was many years later. That memory planted the seeds of bitterness that Hartford managed to nurture. Never again did I feel safe with anyone but my mother and Ulrich. If it weren't for my father, I might not have been so adversely affected by Hartford's antics. But the fact that Hartford even wanted to cheat may have turned me into a real monster, one that had much more power than my father and was not scared of anything.

Looking back at that defining memory, I think that if it weren't for my mother, I would have gone off the deep end right then and there. My mother, along with Ulrich, helped stabilize my emotions and thoughts and allowed me to have a mostly normal childhood. However, even they could not restore my sense of safety when I was among strangers. As a result, I stayed friendless and wandered the streets of Leipzig bottled up in my own thoughts, constantly on the lookout.

Contrary to what Hartford might have thought, I did not consider him a friend. I only considered him a tentative thread to the outside world. I clung to him only because I had no one else even remotely close to my age to cling to, and I needed some sort of stabilizing presence having the same level of intellect as I had.

Hartford definitely had the intellectual capabilities to guide me in the right direction and help me erase the bitterness from my soul. However, his cunning, dirty personality got the better of him, and by copying Hartford's every action, combined with the bitterness I felt, I became the person that I still am today.

Only my mother had kept me from going off the deep end during Hartford's cheating exploits, but she died when I was eleven, still suffering from the injuries she had sustained from my father's rage. He had shattered all the bones in the right side of her face and caved in her skull, making her dangerously ill for the rest of her life. At least she had still been able to teach me the art of persuasion.

Soon after my mother had died, so did Ulrich, and the only two stabilizing forces I had had in my life were gone forever. I went to live with Hartford for a while. However, my mother could no longer stop me from boiling over, and living with Hartford for almost a year and a half drove me dangerously close to the brink.

Oh, if only I had been able to reconcile myself when I had been young and achieve complete inner peace. None of this would have ever happened, and perhaps I would have had a wide net of friends that I could have used to peacefully reform the world. Why had I turned to Hartford, of all people, as a friend? I had basically turned into a carbon copy of him because of my need to latch on to anyone I could find.

I realized that I was the basis for all this, and that fact nearly drove me into insanity. I even became suicidal in my sleep. I realized that if I hadn't been born, there would have been no bitterness, no scandal with my father, no horrible memories, no Tyrannei, no pain, and no psychological scars.

That had driven me to the point at which I wanted to just end it all. I reconciled myself, however, through my enduring hatred for Hartford and my need to see him dead. But without a goal, I would be a shell of my former self, racked by bouts of depression that would overrun me and make me a sobbing heap. I could not let that happen.

That one memory had led to so many things and taught me so much from one single concept, but the second phase of my life had been triggered by another memory: Hartford's acceptance to MIT and my subsequent meeting with Klatschnikov, which formed Tyrannei and drove my creative energy, giving me something to live for.

16

BIRTH OF A NEMESIS

Karl von Liebnitz, his memory at the age of thirteen

I had grown from my quirky two-year-old self to the smartest thirteen-year-old in the world. I had a "friend" in Will Hartford. We had applied for the only opening at MIT that year, and I was on the brink of being accepted to my dream college. It seemed as if my life had turned around from that horrible time when I had been a toddler.

Below the surface, however, there lurked some dark aspects of my life. My mother had died almost two years ago, and her death still cast a dark shadow over my heart. Will Hartford was not a person I could even consider an ally anymore. His cheating had reached new heights. I was afraid that my robot sent to MIT had been sabotaged because I had to borrow microchips from Hartford. Without the calming effect of my mother, I was close to the boiling point.

I was sitting next to him, patiently waiting for the message to arrive from the far-off MIT servers. "Well," I said, forcing a smile, "today the decision comes in. I guess we'll see which of us got in." Hartford smiled back at me. His smile was more like a grimace. "Yes," he replied, "we will see." Then he looked down, and I could see him trying not to laugh. I decided not to say anything, and he looked back up again.

I could tell that he was about to say something, but just as he opened his mouth to speak, the computer dinged, indicating that a new message had arrived in the inbox. "The message is here," said Hartford, failing to contain his victorious ecstasy. "It says that I've been accepted. Sorry, man. Maybe next time."

Hartford looked at me, hoping for a reassuring smile from me. He wanted to hear that the decision was fine and that I could try again later. Oh, the fool. This had happened too many times. I was not going to let this slip by again. Too many times had I ignored his antics and said nothing. My father's genetics kicked in, and I didn't just boil over; I spontaneously exploded.

"First off, *friend*," I said in a chilling, mocking voice. "Don't ever call me 'man' again, Hartford. Second, *congratulations* on your *victory, big fat cheater.*" Hartford stiffened. "Whoa, whoa, whoa," he began, but I cut him off. "Do you know how much I've suffered having you—an insufferable, ruthless, cutthroat prick—as a friend?" I yelled. "Can you even begin to understand in that shriveled brain of yours? Can you?

"Every day since that first competition when I was six, every day you have tried to cut corners and beat me at any cost. You call that part of a friendship? Maybe that's why you're universally hated, scumbag. Have you ever thought about it that way? I know the microchips you gave me were defective. Are you too chicken to think that you can't win by following the rules, that you have to backstab the only person who actually has human interactions with you in a meaningful way?

"You have no morals, fool, and that fact will come back and stab you in the back later in life. You can win your little victories, but they're all Pyrrhic victories, *friend*. I'm breaking off relations with you, you dirty punk. Don't even try to make a comeback!"

I wheeled around and started walking away, intending to leave Hartford forever and never come back again, no matter what he tried to do. Of course Hartford couldn't keep his big fat mouth shut, and he just had to reply to my damning insults. "Karl," he growled, swelling up like a bloated balloon, "take back your insults. Now. Or I will make you pay with our friendship."

I ignored Hartford's appeals. "Good," I shouted back. "That was the goal of my very true rant about your very inferior qualities. Perhaps I should have added that your hubris blinds you from having a clear view of your mistakes." Hartford, since he was Hartford, still had to have the last word though.

"Really, Karl?" he said with a disdainful laugh. "I'm the person who is blinded by his hubris? Look who's talking. All of these years, Karl, I've had to withstand your petty complaints about my unintentional accidents during our meetings in competitions. I've had to remind you time and time again that accidents happen. But still you are blinded by your hubris. In return, you intentionally caused 'accidents' to win competitions that I otherwise would have won. I honestly think, with my unshrouded mind and beliefs, that *you*, Karl, actually are deserving of the very names that you called *me*, the innocent one. Break off our friendship then. I know that you need it as much as I do. Otherwise, you will have no purpose in life and will commit suicide. But the die has been cast."

I tried not to look back, but my emotions were too much for me to handle. "Oh, Hartford," I shouted. "Now that we've broken off our friendship, I do in fact have a purpose in life: I want to murder you for driving the wedge ever deeper and driving me down the wrong path in life, you useless shepherd." I had so much raw emotion that I was able to use my mental powers before even knowing what they were. This allowed me to let my rage break down the barriers that separated the parts of my brain from each other. Slamming my hands forward into thin air, I sent a tidal wave of mental energy crashing into the wall that Hartford was sitting under with his computer. The wall disintegrated, burying Hartford and his computer.

I knew Hartford wasn't dead because his crushed computer would have notified the police that something was wrong, but I knew I hurt him badly. This set the stage for our rivalry. I left Hartford's house quickly. I was now officially homeless as well as friendless.

I wandered through the streets, wishing I could have killed Hartford right then and there, ending this once and for all. Suddenly, however, the full implications of my actions came crashing down on me. I had nobody to help me or be my companion. I was homeless and destitute. I would be dead before the night was out. Street fighting was not my forte.

The events that happened next seemed to be a miracle, making me wonder if God really did exist and if he played a role in what happened. A sixteen-year-old Russian youth walked up to me with a concerned expression on his face. Instantly I grew scared. I thought he was trying to lure me into a fight because he looked tough and could probably beat me in about ten seconds.

Instead he gave me comfort by somehow managing to hit all the right notes, talking about all the right topics, and garnering my grudging support of him. Even he looked shocked at his masterful performance of persuasion. Although I rebuffed him at first, gradually he filled the void in my heart that had been left by Hartford.

He even offered me a place to sleep in his home. As we went there, he told me his story. "My parents are…," he began, struggling to say the next few words, "abusive, to say the least." I nodded in agreement. "I know what you mean. My father was also abusive. He gave me psychological scars at age two." I was so desperate for companionship that I was already pouring out the contents of my soul to this Russian I had just met.

"Luckily," he continued, "my parents are both locked in the asylum, but I got ownership of the house, as stated in the original deed, even though I was only fourteen. So I have the whole place to myself now, along with you. There's not that much space, but it's better than living on the streets."

I silently agreed with him but did not have time to reply out loud because we had arrived at his home. As he had said, it was quite small and would be a tight fit, but it was home nevertheless. The Russian cleared his throat. "Well, this is my home," he said meekly. "By the way, the name's Klatschnikov. Yuri Klatschnikov."

"Nice to meet you, Mr. Klatschnikov," I said. He instantly

looked mortified. "No, no, no," he replied quickly. "Call me Yuri." I shrugged. "OK, Yuri. My name's Karl von Liebnitz. Just call me Karl." Klatschnikov looked at me questioningly but decided not to probe further.

We entered his home, and Klatschnikov hurried to the kitchen to throw together a quick dinner. "You know how to cook?" I asked in admiration. Klatschnikov shrugged. "Yes, it's honestly not that big of a deal. When you live on your own, you learn how to do many basic household chores. Money can only stretch so far."

Klatschnikov pointed to the living room. "You can sleep on one of the couches tonight," he said. "There are blankets and linens in the closet. Tomorrow I'll fix you up a real bed with a real mattress and everything. Well, I guess we don't need to travel back to that street corner for a meeting tomorrow, do we? We can just have it at home."

"Yes," I said in agreement, "we can discuss all that right here tomorrow. How about we just concentrate on eating dinner and going to sleep? Then we can approach the problem with fresh minds." Klatschnikov's kindness had made me forget all about the original reason I had accepted his kindness. His nonchalant statement sobered me back up.

Once dinner was ready, we ate quickly and quietly. I was so tired that I collapsed onto the couch in the corner nearest to the kitchen and fell asleep instantly. Apparently, Klatschnikov put linens and blankets on the couch while I was sleeping, for when I woke up, I was swathed in blankets, and there were linens underneath my leaden body.

"Ah, you're awake," came Klatschnikov's voice from the kitchen as I blearily stumbled in. "I could tell that something very stressful happened to you yesterday because you instantly fell asleep, as if you were trying to sleep off the stress. I won't ask what happened, but I brewed some strong tea to make you feel a bit better."

"Thank you," I said appreciatively, touched by his small signs of affection. I wondered what could have happened to move me from one stable situation to the next so quickly. The celerity of the change was the only thing that amazed me. I slowly sipped my tea, feeling as if all of my stress had just suddenly melted away. The feeling was extraordinary.

"This tea," I said between sips, "is simply amazing! How are you so good at making tea?" Klatschnikov looked off into the distance, reminiscing, and I knew not to probe further. "I had to learn how to brew tea because I've needed it myself many times," he said, his mind obviously in another time and place. I was truly astonished by our coincidental meeting. "Two tortured souls," I began, "somehow find each other in an alley, and now they prepare a plot to reform the world in their own image."

Klatschnikov nodded. "Indeed," he agreed. "I find that the odds of us meeting are finite but still quite small. I feel that perhaps some other being is involved in our meeting. Anyway, we have no time to theorize about omniscient beings. Let us get down to business." Klatschnikov and I sat down for breakfast, and so began the formation of Tyrannei.

17

THE GREAT PLOT TO CLEANSE THE WORLD

Karl von Liebnitz, continuation of memory

As we were settling in to begin our discussion, I tried to sort out my confused thoughts about Klatschnikov. I was bewildered by his behavior. He was known by reputation to be one of the most violent teenage criminals in the streets, hardened by even more brutal parents than mine. He took out his reserve of anger on anyone who managed to annoy him. But now Klatschnikov was acting as if he had an alter ego that was full of benevolence. It was as if he took mercy upon my wretched soul and helped me out from deep inside his own shattered soul.

But if Klatschnikov was not completely in control of himself, did that mean he would revert to his savage mannerisms as soon as we formed our organization? Well, considering the facts, that could actually be a good thing—to have a brutal killing machine on my side that I could deploy at any time and use to power my way to victory. But first we needed to actually establish the organization.

"So," I said, trying to give him the initiative in the beginning, "what should we start with?" As I had hoped, Klatschnikov replied, "We should establish some of our goals and write down a short manifesto about our organization. We should look short term *and* long term when considering our list of goals." I mentally confirmed my suspicions. Klatschnikov's plan was smart and simple to carry out, but I could not believe he had come up with it that quickly in his normal state. Was a miracle happening before my eyes?

"Good idea," I replied. "Do you have any goals that you want to put on the table for discussion?" Klatschnikov thought for a moment and said, "Sure, why not? I have a few short-term goals and a long-term goal I'd like to discuss." If Klatschnikov came up with some brilliant goals, I thought, I must be witnessing some form of mind control. "Fire away," I said, leaning back and preparing to listen.

"OK then," began Klatschnikov. "First off, we need to find a way to recruit some volunteers who agree with our organizational ideals and have the mind-set and potential to be great assets for us. Once we've laid down that foundational core and garnered some successes, the recruits will come flooding in. To recruit members, I suggest writing a stirring manifesto that can utterly convince them that we have the potential to do great things. This, combined with personal recruiting, should help us acquire a few like-minded radicals."

A brilliant idea, I thought, but not Klatschnikov's. Who

wanted to control his mind? "Second," continued Klatschnikov, "we stand to gain hardy fighters who can be put on a tight leash by our core recruits if we break the prisoners out of the asylums. They are probably the people who hate Merkel the most in Germany. This will help us move toward our third goal, which is conquering Germany and starting the reforms we will state in our manifesto. I only have one long-term goal: conquer the earth and make it our own."

I was impressed by the ideas of the person who spoke through Klatschnikov. He or she was concise and on point. However, I had some more goals of my own that I wanted to add. "Yuri," I said calmly, "I thoroughly agree with every single one of your goals. I could not have said it better myself. I would like to expand on your ideas for recruitment and add a long-term goal.

"To increase the number of capable recruits, we also have to get some people who can hack into the news stations around the world and broadcast our message, reaching a wider audience. Along with releasing the lunatics from the asylums, we should increase our global viewership by brutally taking over the streets of Germany. Now, a long-term goal: kill Will Hartford."

I became still again, waiting for Klatschnikov's reply. Slowly he began to speak. "Karl," he said, slightly shocked, "I feel that you are presenting some great and some mediocre ideas. Now that I know who you are, I also know your reputation. It precedes you through the streets. In contrast to me, you were never one of the violent types. When did you become so violent? I feel that your judgment is being clouded by the recent events in your life.

"Your first point about recruitment is a valid one, and we should start instituting that as soon as we recruit some able hackers. However, your other goals and ideas concern me. Why would you want to brutally institute a crackdown when you can win over the populace through persuasion and turn the people against the Merkel dynasty without spilling an excess amount of blood? Do you want to murder our organization before it even springs into existence?

"Regarding Will Hartford, I simply cannot see the point of making that a goal in our manifesto. I don't know what you have against Hartford and why you hate him so much, but I think this goal also ties into your newfound violent personality. We cannot and must not let personal vendettas stand in the way of our glory."

As I look back on that day, I think that I too must have been under some form of mind control, for I exploded in front of Klatschnikov, endangering our newfound friendship and the fate of our organization. "Why are you opposing me so vehemently?" I hissed through gritted teeth. "You should be the one wholeheartedly lending support to my ideas, you fool. You're the violent personality, and I thought that I was appealing to your interest by introducing these recruitment goals.

"Killing Hartford doesn't need to be a goal in our manifesto. However, he is important not only because I hate the slimy snake but because he is the single most important person who will be able to stand in our way. He will be our enemies' rallying point, their beacon of hope, and he will be the only one who will have a chance to foil our carefully thought-out plans."

I must have thought that I was appealing to Klatschnikov's

inner self, but I seemed to be quite mistaken on that point. "Shut up, Karl," he replied with a note of finality in his voice. "Shut up before I rip your head off." My judgment was clouded by anger to the point that I decided to make a comeback of my own. "Go ahead and try, puny weakling," I snarled back. My fleeting jab hit home. Klatschnikov turned purple and charged toward me like a bull.

Without knowing what I was doing, I raised up a hand and pushed forward. Klatschnikov was hit by an invisible force so hard that he split the table in two and crashed into his kitchen wall, debris raining down on him. I walked over and looked down at him. "I'm stronger than you, Yuri," I said in a surprisingly calm voice. "You just can't tell from my external appearance.

"I'm the leader of Tyrannei, the organization that we're going to form. You are second in command. We are not equal partners. I have the smarts to build up Tyrannei into what you picture it to be, and you have the brute strength needed to enforce my orders. I'm accepting your goals and incorporating mine into them. Now we're going to write up the manifesto. Got it?"

Klatschnikov nodded mutely, but I could see the anger smoldering in his eyes, a combination of my treatment of him and him not being able to get payback. I knew that I had most likely just made a potentially dangerous enemy but one that I could probably keep in check. He ripped himself out of the wall with a tearing sound, leaving a Klatschnikov-shaped imprint behind. "Fine," he muttered, clearly deflated from the rough treatment. "Let's get working on the manifesto."

We sat back down at the remnants of his table. With a wave

of my hand, the table fixed itself. Unconsciously, Klatschnikov twitched slightly in surprise. Was that supposed to make me less suspicious? Or did the person controlling Klatschnikov actually not know about this? Well, maybe. After all, I hadn't known what I could do until I hurt Hartford the previous day. Klatschnikov got up and pulled a sheet of paper and a ball-point pen from a cabinet and carefully set them down on the table. I took the pen and wrote "Tyrannei" at the top in big, bold letters.

"Tyrannei," I began out loud while simultaneously writing down what I was saying, "is an organization that was established through a series of events that caused Karl von Liebnitz, the leader of Tyrannei, to act on his ideas. Formed by Merkel haters, this organization's goals include toppling the dictatorship that has had a stranglehold on German politics for nearly three decades.

"We plan to do this by recruiting capable, like-minded volunteers who will give us the resources needed to bring 'Emperor' Merkel III to his knees. This will happen through the dissemination of anti-Merkel propaganda and brutal street battles that will tear down the strongholds of Merkelism one by one. Why do we not persuade the German people to fight Merkel if we make him out to be a snobbish dictator? Because they are the ones who elected him, and they are as much at fault as Merkel is. Violence will make them learn to keep their mouths shut and join our cause.

"We plan to strike fear in the hearts of all Germans by unleashing hell on them. You may ask yourselves, what is Tyrannei thinking? Where could they possibly get hell from? Well, Tyrannei has an answer for you. You must have heard about Merkel's famous asylums by now. You must have also heard rumors about what they do to the inmates there. In those hell houses stay the most hard-core opponents of Merkel, even if some of them seem deranged.

"Now, we ask you, what do you think will happen when we release these raving lunatics into German streets? We think you know the answer to that by now. It will be hell for you ordinary Germans who decided to vote for Merkel. Don't you regret that seemingly inconsequential decision now?

"After we conquer Germany and utilize its vast resources to our advantage, we will also institute beneficial reforms to create a strong and prosperous Germany for all ordinary Germans to revel in. What would be next on our list? Well, that would be conquering the entire earth and forcing our reforms upon it, of course.

"You see, the earth is inherently corrupt at its very core. It is like a sick man who refuses to let go of life and die. It clings to whatever refuge it can find and endeavors to find a way to keep going. This doesn't sound so bad until these corrupt tendrils strike into the very hearts of the ruling class. Then we have a definite problem on our hands. These leaders corrupt the world daily and bring the human race closer to extinction with their imbecilic actions. We must step in and save humanity from being drowned in a shallow pond when there is a way out.

"The above words are our goals and our explanations for them. We intend to accomplish them in the manner listed above and hope that like-minded individuals from around the world will join us in our race against time to save the poor humans, who are suffocating because of the very place they call home. Signed, Karl von Liebnitz, leader of Tyrannei, and Yuri Klatschnikov, second in command of Tyrannei."

I stopped writing with a satisfied expression. I had poured my heart and soul into this document, and I felt that I had created a masterful piece of writing. I asked Klatschnikov, "Well, I want an honest answer: What do you think of the manifesto?" He replied without hesitation. "Your rhetoric and deft use of language are amazing, Karl," he said with adoration in his voice. "I think we have just made history."

I smiled triumphantly and signed my name on the manifesto with a flourish. I handed the pen to Klatschnikov. He signed as well. "Well," I said, "now we need to scan this and create a digital master copy so we can print tens of thousands of copies to post all over Germany. Then it will be time to go recruiting."

Klatschnikov agreed with me, and so Tyrannei began. We really did make history on that day. We really did. We set the world on a crash course with death. But was that what I really wanted now?

Suddenly I realized that my voyage into my past was over and that I was being sucked back into the present. Ideas that were foreign to me began to sweep through my head as I saw my naive self flash back in front of my eyes. Then all went black and I was back in the operating room.

18

IDEALS PREVAIL

Karl von Liebnitz

I awoke to see Heinz standing over me with a concerned look. "Meister," he asked anxiously, "are you OK?" Inwardly I was groaning, but I maintained a tranquil composure on the outside. I was flooded by emotions that I had not felt in a long time. I felt...was that regret? And shock at my own actions? Had viewing those memories induced a change in my inner sanctum?

I had to fight these feelings. I had to focus on an important issue that would bring forth my usual mix of emotions. Then I remembered what was happening. The three resistance fighters had escaped, but I was tracking them. They had probably landed at their base by now. I had to destroy their base as soon as possible. The drones were already deployed, ready for the task at hand.

I sprang up suddenly and spasmed with pain. Heinz rushed into my path and tried to protect me. "Nein, Meister!" he shouted. I ignored him and ran to the controls of the drones. I did not feel ready for infiltration of the base, but I had to take my mind off the memories.

The video feed from the drones was already streaming onto the control screen. After a few clumsy attempts with the drones' weapons, I finally opened the door to the hidden hangar. Jackpot! I saw their Turbojet parked beneath the opening in the landing position with the doors opened. They must be there. No doubt about it.

I pushed down on the controls and the drones descended. I looked around. Then I realized my grave mistake. No way had I been played a fool for the second time. They had built a hangar and nothing more. They had presumably switched ships and were far out of my limited range. Another stupid mistake. I cursed under my breath.

"Foligno!" I called out. "Ja, Meister?" came the reply. "Send orders to Klatschnikov to come back to headquarters immediately, no matter the circumstances. Send out a message to the rest of the commanders to prepare for an imminent battle." Foligno nodded. "Of course, Meister, I will do what you request immediately." Since I could not catch Hartford and company, there would be a humongous bloody battle. With that thought, the foreign feelings that had lingered in me since awaking from the surgery evaporated, and I began my battle preparations with a shadow lifted off my shoulders.

Pierre Hartford

Eventually we arrived at our final destination. I slowed the Osprey to a gentle stop and let it glide downward. Mentally I unlocked the hangar doors, and an opening appeared beneath us. The Osprey deployed its landing gear, and we landed with a gentle thump. A hatch opened and we stepped out into our new home.

From another hatch, the boxes containing the paper files were unloaded. "We need to secure these files immediately," said Mr. Roland. "They could win us the war." Dad and I quickly moved the files to the vault.

After the files had been secured, the three of us sat down for a roundtable discussion. There was an awkward silence that I finally decided to break. "Well," I said quietly, "aren't we going to discuss our next move?"

Mr. Roland slowly replied, "Well, whether or not Liebnitz has tracked us, he is going to prepare for an imminent battle. That means we must prepare as well.

"We have a massive stockpile of weapons, including the one that Pierre designed with teleporting bullets, under our command. Along with that, we also have twenty divisions of elite shock troopers, the invaluable files in the vault, an aging air force at our disposal, and our three brilliant minds with their respective abilities."

As Mr. Roland finished talking, I looked around the table to gauge the temperature of the water. I knew that internally I was worn out and being torn in half, but externally I looked calm. Mr. Roland, on the other hand, looked as if he had aged twenty years in a single day. The hostage crisis involving his family must really be hitting him hard, I thought.

On the other hand, Dad's face was stoic. I could not glean anything from my cursory glance at him. I guessed that he must have been worn out as well from all of this stress and action. But perhaps he was simmering with anger at his childhood friend. Dad could sometimes be quite volatile in his own right. I hoped that he was not in such a foul mood that he could derail everything.

"Sir," I said to Mr. Roland, "since we're going to be commencing preparations, perhaps I should design some more weapons and the like to give to these shock troopers. The weapons that I have seen them carry on regular duty are woefully inadequate for the job we have ahead of us. Hopefully, we also have a few sets of armor to give to the especially skilled troopers and officers."

"Yes," replied Mr. Roland, "that's a great idea. Will and I could also jointly prepare the troopers, distribute the weapons and armor we already have lying around, and look through the vault for the vital information that might let us bring Liebnitz to his knees." I agreed with that proposal immediately. We seemed ready to get to our individual duties when Dad spoke up.

"No," he said flatly, "I'm not playing games with you anymore, Christian. I'm done with your stupid organization. Unless you want to betray your government, I don't think I can work with you any longer." Mr. Roland and I were confused. "What in the world are you talking about, Will?" replied Mr. Roland with a note of astonishment in his wavering voice.

"You think you don't know what I'm talking about, Christian?" said Dad with venomous disbelief dripping with every syllable. "I think you should have a pretty good idea what I'm talking about. After all, you do put up with their stupid orders day after day, week after week, month after month, year after year.

"I expressed very clearly to you at the beginning that I would not fight with you in this war if I had to be in direct collaboration with the very symbols of power I hate so vehemently. Did you think that I would change my mind and, in the process, my ideals? If you did, I must really say that you are too naive to be in the position that you are in right now, Christian.

"You know that I hate the US government and governments like it with all of my heart and soul. They are bloated and overstretched pieces of junk, overseen by arrogant figureheads who do nothing to stop the disease that is making the earth rotten from the core outward. That blight is called the vices of humanity. Every day, we grow ever more selfish and care more about ourselves than we do about others. The government does nothing to stop this. In fact, it helps this cause along, speeding up the extinction of humanity in the process.

"You think that I would really want to keep a piece of junk like that in the seat of power by helping you defeat my greatest nemesis, Karl von Liebnitz? If anything, Pierre and I should be in the seat of power, reforming our planet to save the people from killing each other. We could stop the disease together, and you could help us, Christian, if you had the courage to break away from the sinking boat that you call your master.

"In this case, I don't think the age-old adage of the enemy of your enemy being your friend holds true. I consider you a tentative source of help in my quest to bring down Karl. To be honest with you, I thought that your entire organization was already far beyond saving, even after your merger with the NSA had made you stronger. In the battle against Tyrannei, your shock troopers stand no chance against Karl's super-soldiers. His strength is far greater than yours will ever be, Christian. Only Pierre and I can stop his inevitable march toward world destruction. So I ask you, Christian, are you brave enough to join Pierre and me in our mission to save the world from your boss, or are you so blindly loyal that you cannot betray your fellow countrymen?"

Dad finished his statement and sat down quietly with the expression of a man waiting for an answer. Mr. Roland had turned white with astonishment, looking as if he would faint. I felt quite troubled now. What made Dad believe that I could join him so willingly and oppose Mr. Roland, the only father figure I've ever had besides him?

"Dad," I began quietly, buying Mr. Roland some more time so that he could compose himself. "What makes you think that I have no moral values all of a sudden? I have never changed my basic personality from what it was since this war started. I am not going to betray Mr. Roland. I, for one, see him as more than a tentative source of help, as you termed it. He's been more of a father to me these past few days than you ever were to me through twenty-one years of my life.

"If, as you say, the US government and governments like it are corrupting the world and killing from the core outward, why not start your reforms there? With enough time and effort, you can reform the entire governmental system of the world and turn it into an efficient bureaucratic democracy, healing the wound that it inflicted upon itself. How do you think the governments will take it if you defeat Liebnitz and then almost immediately decide to alienate them? You will be hurting no one but yourself, Dad.

"For the love of God, please don't leave, Dad. We are stronger together than if you decide to abandon us. I'm not going to go with you. Maybe this is why nobody can be friends with you. I've finally realized that my father is the biggest hypocrite I know. For all of your talk of the world corrupting itself and humanity driving itself to extinction, you can't and don't seem to realize that you are a slimy, corrupt snake that cannot be trusted under any circumstances. It's sad, but if you leave, I will be forced to take up arms against you in the future. So please, don't weaken the resistance against Tyrannei when that's the last thing we need."

I sat down and Mr. Roland slowly stood up. "Will," he said with a bitter twinge in his voice, "for many, many years, I thought you were my friend. I see now that I was mistaken. I was only a pawn in your measly chess game to 'save' the world. From what, you say? Corrupt people and governments. How can you say that when you yourself are corrupt? I cannot abandon my government. Pierre does have a point. We could reform the government from the inside out. Please consider that, Will, and don't make us lose out to Tyrannei."

After listening to these two impassioned pleas for him to change his mind, Dad stood up abruptly, his face darkening quickly. "Fine then," he muttered. "If neither of you wants a thing to do with me, I'll just pack up and leave."

I felt a great sadness at having Dad leave, but my morals told me that I should not be near such a slimy snake. However, I was afraid that Dad was going to do something impulsive and stupid.

He turned toward the door and began to walk out. Just before he was out of sight, I had blocked his mental powers, in case he had wanted to do something dumb. Dad felt my mental shield around him, and he snapped. "Pierre," he growled, "you are being extremely stupid. Stop it right now." I countered with equal determination, "I cannot let you sabotage our mission, Dad. This is for your own good."

"*Shut up!*" roared my father. "I can do whatever I want. I'm not the one who is corrupt; it's all of you fools! I don't understand it. Why can't you just betray the US government?" Dad apparently thought he had talked enough, for he let out a humongous roar, and with a concentrated blast of energy, he broke through my mental bonds and teleported out of the base.

The shock wave from his blast of energy slammed through my mental defenses and smashed the room apart. Apparently, rage was quite a volatile fuel for mental energy. Dad had actually gone and done it. He had betrayed us and left us a wreck, stupidly deciding to fight a hopeless war on two fronts.

I let out a whimper as my brain struggled to cope with the immense pain flooding through me. I was weeping, I realized, and I felt weak for the first time in my life. But I could not let my anger overtake me, or we were truly a lost cause. I had to deal with this, and Mr. Roland and I would be able to win the war against Tyrannei. First, though, I needed to fix myself up.

19

THE STORM GATHERS

Will Hartford

All of them were demons, every single last one of them. First it had been foolish Karl von Liebnitz, who had turned into a megalomaniac and was taking over the world. Then it was poor Christian, who had been naive enough to believe that I would actually help the very thing that I sought to destroy for the sake of humanity. Even my son had turned into one of the minions of the devilish disease. In the end, he turned on me for the "greater good." No one else could be the greater good. I was the greater good.

Abandoned and forsaken, I was left to fend for myself in the hostile environment found outside of my sanctum. All of this evil was overwhelming me to the point that I could not control my mental powers, and this had caused the great explosion with Pierre. If I kept on going, I would burn myself out and turn into an empty shell, forcing me to start all over again from square one.

I could not let that happen. The healing light had to prevail over the swallowing tightness of the dark. I had to go out into the world as a beacon of healing. But to know one's enemy, one had to act like one's enemy. One could not fight devils with angels over and over again and hope to win in the end. New tactics had to be used to defeat the ever-adapting enemy. One can only win the arms race by staying one step ahead of the enemy.

Now was the time for me to pull myself together and get used to the feeling of working without allies. I always was abandoned when the tables were turned against me. Then they saw my true holiness for what it really was. I needed to keep the light at the end of the tunnel in sight; I could not let the demons break through my defenses and take over, plunging the world into eternal darkness. What would mankind do then? There was nothing people could do against that. That's why I needed to stand before the demons and wage the final great battle to bring them down.

I had teleported out of the base impulsively and stupidly, utterly forgetting to take any valuable files or anything else they could use against me when we met on a battlefield. See, this is what happened when I let my impulses take over. Bad things always happened. That impassioned speech had almost convinced them of my righteousness, but my loss of control had driven them out of my reach and into the arms of the conniving enemy.

They had all betrayed me. All of the people I thought were friends had turned into enemies. I was being pushed into a corner. I would sadly have to smash them up to break out and fulfill my ultimate vision. Without it, how could the world survive? I could not see that happening. They needed me, the man who could save the day, to come in and stop the disease.

Where was I, anyway? It seemed that I had teleported myself through my rage to the place that I held most dear to my heart. I had returned to Hungary, where I had spent the years of my life that I loved best. There I had started my resistance campaign by letting Cybor die. I had let its entire hierarchy change so I could take it over without dealing with sniveling old men.

I had fallen in love with Pierre's mother here. Pierre had been born here. Oh, how good those days had been. It had all been before I started manipulating people to begin the resistance. All in all, perhaps it had been a mistake to have humanity try to help itself out of its own hole. After all, everything that humanity tried to fix only got worse after its intervention.

I shook myself out of my thoughts and looked around at my peaceful home. It had not changed since I had left it last. It had stayed the same through the years, as if it were expecting me to come back one day. At least my house was on my side. Then I remembered. I had left my entire computer system here when I had departed, just in case I ever had to come back after being sent into exile.

That system was pure gold to me. With it, I would be able to take down all of my enemies with ease. Karl wouldn't know what was coming for him, and neither would Pierre and Christian. I did not know what they held in the vault, but I hoped that it was nothing damning about me. I knew my own flaws very well, and I knew that if they found out about those flaws, there was nothing I could do to save humanity from a slow, painful death.

Why couldn't I just go back to the days when I had been happy all the time, even in the resistance movement? What change had come over me? It had not been Karl, for I had been happy for many years after Karl had turned evil. When did I become so angry and hateful and full of hopelessness? I tried to think back, but it was as if my memory had been wiped. It was as if an iron curtain separated me from my memories of just a few years ago.

What was happening? Was I really losing my touch and turning old? Perhaps people could only take so much loss. I felt I had reached my ultimate limit and could go no further. No wonder I had snapped after that ultimate insult on my character. I drove away my nostalgia and concentrated on my anger, letting my rage take over and become a driving force so that I could finish what I had started more than twenty years ago.

Suddenly a mental presence that was pure evil over-whelmed my defenses and took over my mind. I tried to fight it off, but it was much stronger than anything I had ever en-countered, even stronger than Pierre. In the end, I succumbed to this demon and blacked out.

Karl von Liebnitz

I could not stop my inevitable change in personality from a sadistic, mindless killing machine with a cutting intelligence and a vitriolic manner of writing to a puny pacifist. I didn't know if my memories exacerbated this change that came over me, but I would never be what Hartford had tried to make me into. Of that, at least, I was sure.

However, I did not feel that these foreign feelings were so bad after all. It was reasonable to expect that you could bring the population onto your side more quickly when you decided not to institute a bloody crackdown on freedom but let freedom flow while maintaining a bureaucratic structure that was not horribly inefficient. You could not truly bring people to your side if you suppressed them.

I, for one, should have known that firsthand. My resentment toward Hartford had been repressed for years and years, and I had become more and more wound up, pressuring the boiling kettle into an even more precarious state. You should not do to others what you would not want to happen to yourself.

Hartford, however, did not deserve any good treatment of this kind, and I felt no difficulty in hating him completely for his insidious poisoning of my entire life, making me a lost soul in the prime of my life. In fact, if it hadn't been for our divergent personalities, we might have reformed the world together. After all, the only thing that held us apart was our hate.

We both wanted the same type of reforms, we both had similar interests, we both had unnatural intelligence, and we both were extremely gifted with mental abilities. It was as if we had broken the strings that dragged us through our time on the earth and had nearly bonded into an unstoppable team. Perhaps we had been jerked back to reality and separated with no chance of reconnecting.

Pierre, however, was even more intellectually gifted than I. However, he might also have been corrupted by his father, which made him somebody with whom I could not work.

Perhaps I was destroying my own reality again by having my entire emotional makeup modified to become more divergent from my organization. I would be able to keep it together for this battle, but what about after that?

Klatschnikov, Bartleby, and Joubert each had a large camp of supporters that probed me constantly for weaknesses. If they sensed that I was losing my grip on power, I would be gone faster than I could blink. I had hired them at a time when it had seemed I would need their ruthlessness to keep my subdued populations in line, but now their power was being turned against me. It was as if my closest advisers were turning into the friends of my greatest enemy.

I was snapped out of my thoughts by the sound of the alarm, indicating that Klatschnikov had returned. He strode into my office and saluted me immediately. "You wanted me back here, Meister?" he asked, sounding a bit bewildered. "Yes, Yuri," I replied. "The search is over. We do not need to search for them. They will come to us. This is because our dear liability, Christian Roland, wants to come rescue his poor, innocent wife and children. Now that they have shaken us off their trail, they will concentrate on engaging us in battle to gain back what the liability has lost."

Klatschnikov nodded, understanding. "But how do you know that they will come to where we want them to come, Meister?" he asked. I had another answer up my sleeve. "Once we begin our mobilization, Yuri, I think it will be very hard for us to hide that obvious fact. After all, have you ever seen or heard of a mobilization on the scale and in the location where we are mobilizing that was unnoticed by the rest of the world?

"Once we are seen mobilizing, we will be able to attract

them to our troops, forcing a battle and snapping shut a trap that will destroy our opposition once and for all. Contrary to popular belief, we do not have the resources to fight a long, drawn-out, defensive war. Neither do our opponents. We will both be searching for a quick knockout punch. We have an advantage in almost every category. With that advantage, we will prevail over their weaker forces."

Klatschnikov suddenly understood my cunning strategy. "I see what you are doing now, Meister," he replied. "You are killing your enemies and making Tyrannei the de facto leader of the world by eliminating both Hartfords and Roland, the trio of thorns in our side." Klatschnikov began to cackle with glee as he realized what would happen after the resistance was defeated. I knew that he was thinking of his contingency plan to overthrow me as well. Perhaps he thought that I would get weaker after a decisive victory and pass on the torch to him.

"Very well," I said, standing up. "Should we gather the rest of the commanders of the Tyrannei forces and look through our arsenals to make sure that everything is in working condition?" Klatschnikov had no choice but to agree with this smart idea, and we walked through the network of corridors to the conference room, where I had already gathered the other commanders.

"Comrades," I announced as I walked in, "we are in the perfect position to do away with Will Hartford, his son, Pierre, and their ally, Christian Roland, all in one stroke. This battle will draw them into the trap I have laid using Christian Roland's wife and children as hostages. This will draw them onto the battleground against our mobilizing army, for they will also be looking for a knockout punch. However, they will not be able to knock us out, for we are Tyrannei, and we are stronger. For Tyrannei we fight! The arsenals will now be checked and the warriors brought out for a final inspection. For the reform of the world!"

My commanders cheered, and we walked through the building, shouting out battle cries. Our coup de grace was about to be revealed, and that would create the vital tipping point for us. No one knew about this new invention except for Tyrannei, and that would spell disaster for the other side in this unfair battle. Nothing could beat us unless they had four aces hidden up their sleeves, which was highly unlikely.

20

COUNTERBALANCE

Pierre Hartford

I was shocked to my core that Dad had gone over the edge in such a startling and rapid fashion. It was, after all, an open secret that Dad was a bit…unstable, to say the least. Dad had some strong emotions about the threat of Tyrannei, but that did not mean he had to throw his "friends" under the bus because they weren't committed enough to taking down Karl von Liebnitz. It was sad and ridiculous that I had to lose my father over this issue, on which he stubbornly refused to bend.

It was as if I had been fighting myself all through my counterspeech to Dad, trying to resist the urge to agree and go with him into the unknown. It was as if my anger had been connected to this unknown force. Did that mean my mind was wired in such a way that I would go off the deep end as Dad had done if I unleashed the full extent of my powers?

That would spell disaster! I would be a useless pawn in the approaching battle.

I was so engrossed in my thoughts that I forgot I was still trying to cope with parts of my brain having been fried, and I realized that I was unconsciously whimpering. Mr. Roland picked himself up out of the rubble and dusted himself off. He looked even worse than I felt, but I did not know the true extent of the damage to my brain. Feebly, I tried to erect a mental shield to block Mr. Roland from trying to fix me up, but I felt a stab of pain and my shield failed almost immediately.

"Pierre," asked Mr. Roland urgently, "what's wrong now?" I groaned inaudibly and gasped, "My brain...fried...certain areas...mental...down for the count." Mr. Roland looked thunderstruck. I didn't know how he could take so much pain and loss in such a short span of time. First he lost his family, then he lost my father, and now he lost me. I could see him frantically trying to formulate a reasonable solution to this problem. The vault would only give us an edge if I was 100 percent ready for the battle.

Suddenly, however, I felt myself losing control of all of my bodily functions. With what felt like a clumsy jerk, I slowly maneuvered into a standing position. Amazingly, I felt no pain at all. Somehow I could feel my fried brain piecing itself back together and returning to normal. My mental shield kicked back in, and Mr. Roland was pushed backward several feet.

Then I regained control of my limbs and almost toppled over from fatigue. Mr. Roland looked even more bewildered then he had looked when I had been lying on the floor. "A miracle?" he sputtered. "What is this? How is this happening, Pierre?" I was just as confused as Mr. Roland sounded. It certainly felt a bit like divine intervention, indicating that I was indeed being controlled by a force beyond my field of vision. "Sir," I replied, "I am just as confused as you are. I feel that a miracle is probably the simplest and best explanation for this phenomenon."

This phenomenon, however, made me wonder. Was I truly doing this out of my own free will? Technically, I was not, for there was no such thing as free will. But was there another being controlling my brain and forcing it into decisions, and had this same being intervened by placing a healing field around me? After all, my brain would know my decisions before the thoughts actually popped into my head. Perhaps I was being hijacked mentally at that stage.

Did that mean my mental powers were just a fluke as well? Did they even exist if it weren't for these unknown beings? Was this all a dream somewhere in the subconscious of one of these superior beings beyond my sight? Did that mean I was actually not on Earth, that there was no battle at all, and that I was just a bubble of subconscious thoughts tangled in the chaotic mass of one of these beings' subconscious? Did I even exist then?

The thought that I did not accomplish all of this scared me. But no, that wasn't possible. After all, mental abilities were just a hidden part of the brain that was unlocked via evolution. My family and Liebnitz were mutations. We had to be. In a few generations, most of humanity would be like this through natural selection, right? We were the few outliers from a slow and steady progression. It was preposterous that this world was anything but real. I would realize that something was wrong if this were a dream. After all, one could not be born in a dream.

I shook off my doubts and addressed Mr. Roland again.

"Sir, you said something earlier about the files we rescued from the vault, that they could win us the war? Perhaps we should look through those very files for that crucial information and then mobilize our forces." Mr. Roland nodded automatically. "Yes, yes," he said absently. "That's a good idea. Come to think of it, there's stuff on Liebnitz as well as your father."

If the information was solid, I thought, we would have more than a fighting chance. We would have a definite chance at beating down Liebnitz, as well as my father. "Let's go then," I replied briskly. Mr. Roland and I walked toward the elevator. He pressed the button for the vault, we got on, and the elevator hurtled all the way to the bottom, two and a half miles down. Before hitting bottom, we slowed to a stop in a matter of seconds.

"You really have been preparing, sir," I said admiringly. "Gravitational elevators are quite finicky and expensive, and having one installed is a big bonus in such a large base." Mr. Roland smiled weakly in response. Almost immediately I felt the warning bells starting to go off in my head. Had Dad done something to Mr. Roland as well, or was this something completely unrelated? You did not get such a weak response from such a great compliment, not even from a humble person. There had to be something wrong with Mr. Roland.

I decided not to press the issue now, however, for I would surely have gotten a fake response, so we walked into the vault. There was quite an advanced system installed for such flimsy files. Each box that had been in the Osprey was sealed in its own clerium compartment, two feet thick on each side. Each compartment, in turn, was inscribed with a number. Clerium interferes with mental abilities just as lead interferes with X-rays. It acts as a shield against mental intrusion, so I could not mentally peer inside the boxes to see which one to open. That meant I had to rely on Mr. Roland, whom I did not completely trust anymore.

As I predicted, the vault was voice controlled. "Box five-thirteen," Mr. Roland said in a monotone that suggested boredom. OK, there was definitely something wrong with him. You did not become bored during such an important mission. You had to stay vigilant if you wanted to live. I didn't want to press my luck just yet, so I waited for the box to appear and open. With a whir, a compartment slid open and one of the boxes I had seen on the Osprey floated out.

"The Liebnitz Papers," said Mr. Roland in his monotone. A robotic screwdriver whirred into position and demagnetized the screws before unscrewing them with a slight buzzing noise. A robotic clamp slid down and picked up the lid, setting it down on the side and out of the way. A smaller clamp riffled through the files and picked up a particularly bulky one, labeled "The Liebnitz Papers" on the side.

I opened the file, pulled out a thick sheaf of papers, and began to riffle through them. The top one began, "Tyrannei Manifesto: Tyrannei is an organization that was established through a series of events that caused Karl von Liebnitz, the leader of Tyrannei, to act on his ideas. Formed by Merkel haters, this organization's goals include toppling the dictatorship that has had a stranglehold on German politics for nearly three decades."

Interesting how one's goals change over time, I thought as I read through the manifesto. It contained subtle hints of what Liebnitz would eventually do, but now Germany had been conquered in the manner described, and he was starting to achieve his long-term goal. The rest of the file contained similar stuff—Tyrannei's timeline, takeovers, recruitment numbers, commanders, blah-blah-blah.

I wondered which spy had access to such extensive information. Not Gurov, I was sure. Was one of Liebnitz's commanders secretly betraying him? Based on what I read, that was not unlikely.

When I finished reading the file, I had noticed two things that could be potential game changers in the fight, but I did not tell Mr. Roland for fear of his untrustworthiness. The first thing I had noticed was something that had been underlined numerous times in various documents:

> Liebnitz is undergoing a continuous power struggle with his commanders, putting him in a vulnerable position if he makes a mistake. Turning the commanders against him might work (?)

The second thing I had noticed was this:

> Liebnitz has recently committed most of his headquarters to a computerized system that he had designed. His system is quite advanced and has proven to be almost impenetrable. However, a skilled mentalist or surface under-bug crawlers could do the trick.

That second fact was particularly promising, in my opinion. If Liebnitz had computerized his system and had been improving upon Cybor's most innovative discoveries as well, he could have created a robotic army vulnerable to the same types of attacks as his system. That could be a decisive advantage to shutting down even part of his army.

Coincidentally, the file after Liebnitz's was labeled "The Hartford Papers." As I looked through it, I found material similar to that in Liebnitz's file. However, one statement stood out to me the most in Dad's file:

> Hartford has known personality issues as well as a hatred of our government. He has a reputation as a cunning snake. Under no circumstances give him your complete trust, or suffer the consequences. His hate of Karl von Liebnitz may be overridden by this most fundamental of all hatreds, meaning we have a potential battle on two fronts.

This fact was extremely shocking to read, especially expressed so frankly by Dad's "allies." I had seen hints of this friction between Mr. Roland and him but not to this extent. Apparently, the trust had been lacking on both sides of the relationship, leading to the opposition's lack of action against Tyrannei and providing that organization with exactly the opportunity it needed to grow.

I snapped the files shut and replaced them in the box, which was instantly carried away by a robotic forklift and sealed up again. I stood up to find Mr. Roland looking at me with an expression of hunger on his face that scared me even more. "Well?" he asked with a leer. "What did you find that will help us in our fight against Tyrannei and your father?" I responded with uncustomary coldness. "None of your business, *sir.* I can handle it on my own."

Mr. Roland's character changed almost immediately. "Give me the information, you little fool!" he roared. I thought sadly, "Why Mr. Roland too?" Then I replied determinedly, "No, I do not give information to beasts like you, foul creature possessing Mr. Roland. I'm not going to even bother and give you false information. I want you out of Mr. Roland right now." Mr. Roland smiled. "Oh, little Pierre," he simpered, "don't you realize? I am puny Mr. Roland. You never knew the real Mr. Roland. Poor little boy, why don't you give me the information before I have to fight you?"

Suddenly I lost control of my body for the second time in a day. "Enough, Alarkabac," I growled. "Give up the game and give the old man his body back. I'm not giving you the information." Mr. Roland/Alarkabac stared at me. "Don't be such a hypocrite, Odlil," he countered. "It's not as if you aren't controlling the boy. Let go of him, and I'll let go of the old man."

I/Odlil threw Alarkabac into the air and pinned him against the wall with a mental burst. "Why should I trust you, slimeball?" I growled. "I was yearning for an excuse to finish you." Alarkabac roared back and threw himself off the wall and out of the strong mental bonds, unleashing bursts of energy at me. I countered all of them. Back and forth they went, using Mr. Roland's body and mine as the vessels through which they fought.

The room trembled as mental energy swirled through the air. Wormholes opened and closed with regularity. Time visibly bent and warped as the air seemed to split into pieces. No one appeared to be gaining the upper hand. Suddenly Odlil unleashed a spell that shook the room. "Be gone, slimeball," he muttered, "even if I must sacrifice myself to stop this madness." With a final roar, he blasted my body apart in midair, unleashing a tidal wave of mental energy that disintegrated the world around me and vaporized Alarkabac as well.

A vortex opened and my soul was sucked in, making me feel as if I were being stretched to an infinite length. The vortex screeched and collapsed on itself. Through and through an endless corridor I hurtled, zooming past infinite files and boxes, and everything I saw around me blurred. Finally I smashed through one of the boxes and was back in control of my body. Mr. Roland popped out as well. With a crash, I fell onto the floor and was knocked unconscious.

21

THUNDERBOLT

Yuri Klatschnikov

The other commanders may have been convinced by this little plan Meister had designed to trap the opposition, but I was not completely convinced that it would work. You could view his announcement as a way of showing strength and keeping us from nipping at his heels while he tried to defeat his nemesis, but not ours. We were Tyrannei, not Liebnitz's Terrorists.

We should act like a group and not like puppets. Meister was not the saving grace that every commander portrayed him to be. I was pretty sure that I was not the only one who had had such an awful first experience with him. Being slammed into a wall is not a pleasant way to start a relationship. It creates weakness for the leader. As soon as he lost his iron grip, he would be pounced on and devoured by people like me.

However, I had still felt pity for him and had even considered him a friend until he started punishing the other commanders as well.

It felt strange, however, to be treated in such a callous manner after I had plucked him off the streets, fed him, and let him recover. If it weren't for me, Tyrannei might not even exist. I still wondered, though, what strange motives could have induced me to comfort Liebnitz. Back then I had been even more of a cutthroat menace than I am now.

It was as if I had been attracted by Liebnitz's repulsive actions because of his "noble" and radical ideas, which were headed in the right direction to fix up this world. Wait a second though. Why was I even pursuing this train of thought anyway? It was as if I was being pushed in strange directions by hidden motives again...no, no, no. It could not be possible. Was I being controlled by something unseen and unheard? Was I an agent of the devil?

I freaked out at the thought of it and began preparing my defenses and gathering weapons. The plan would not work if I was unreliable and out of commission. But Meister needed me, and I needed him to complete my own goals for my own purposes. Should I ring the alarm? After all, Meister would probably know what to do with mental menaces. He was, after all, one himself.

Suddenly a peal of laughter rang through the room. "Not so fast with that alarm, Mr. Klatschnikov. It would be in your best interest to hold off and listen up to what I have to say. I do say, though, you have an interesting thought process, Mr. Klatschnikov, and your conclusions are not as wrong as one would think, considering you. If anybody is a menace, though, it's probably my greatest enemy not called Karl but the devils infesting *my* world."

I looked around wildly, trying to locate the source of that snide voice. Why did I feel as if I recognized that voice from somewhere before? And since when could the air read my thoughts? Assuming that this *thing*, if that's what it was, was part of the air, rendering its presence invisible to me. "Oh, I'm not the air, Mr. Klatschnikov. I exist in the flesh in *this* place, at least. You might recognize the vessel I am using though," continued that slithering voice.

Out of the shadows appeared a man who looked fleetingly familiar to me. He wore plain, drab clothes and looked a bit worn out, but there was a glimmer of a taunting smile floating at the edges of his lips. Suddenly the pieces clicked together, and I realized whom I was staring at. "Will Hartford!" I gasped, realizing that the resistance must have split or I was being lured into a trap for Hartford to be so bold and impudent.

"Correct, Mr. Klatschnikov," replied Hartford. "However, that is only the name of the vessel I am using to accomplish my goals. Come now, you must know who I really am behind this mask. I am one of the few people who can see the entirety of your soul. I know what you yearn for, and you have hoped for me for many years now. You know me almost as well as you know Karl, Yuri Sergeyevich Klatschnikov."

I gasped in shock as recognition poured down upon me. "G…G…God?" I stammered. "But you're not su…supposed to reveal yourself to us mortals. I'm astounded that you are honoring me in such a glorious manner." Hartford/God waved me to stop. "Enough," he said. "I didn't come here to listen to an imbecile's stammering glorifications of what humanity considers me. You petty beings may consider me God, although I am not really God in the true sense of the word.

"You see, this entire world is what one might call...one-sided. If we let you petty beings of consciousness off the leash, this fiasco is what happens. I warned Odlil that this would happen if he loosened his grip on his spin-offs. So my companions and I decided to take matters into our own hands and start turning this subconscious incubator into a reasonable bubble of universal experimentation.

"That means we are here to stage an intervention. You will obey us, for you will be one of the tools we use to regain control of this world without a fight from your petty criminal personalities. You try and do anything to us, and we'll just shut you down. I'm warning you, Yuri Sergeyevich Klatschnikov; if you resist, you will not be pleased with the resulting mess you will make. What say you? Are you going to listen to God, or are you going to commit a grievous sin?"

I stiffened my internal resistance almost instantly. This could not be God. God was not this cruel and evil. God was merciful, loving, and caring. God was not so offhand about punishment and hate. Even if he said he was not truly God, he was not even close to being God. My face tightened and I hissed with an expression of extreme coldness, "You, creature possessing Hartford, are not the God I know.

"When I knew God, he was merciful and helpful. He would listen and give me advice on my problems. He would forgive me. He was my stronghold in the roaring sea. You, on the other hand, are some joke that one of my many enemies has played on me. You are a conjurer and a fake. Even a fool could see you for what you truly are: the demonic opposite of everything that

God stands for. You are the ideological opposite of God. I name you an incarnation of my demonic brain: Fakery."

Hartford stiffened. "Oh, Yuri Sergeyevich Klatschnikov," he growled with a slight tone of regret. "I gave you a chance to let me save you. I gave you your chance to do that. Now, unfortunately, I must, as I phrased it earlier, shut you down."

With a sudden rush of charged energy, the room disintegrated. Hartford's wave of energy threatened to overwhelm me. Suddenly I lost control of my body as another being like Hartford possessed me and pushed back the mental energy. "You will not turn him to your cause," the being inside me promised. "We agreed after your foolish meddling that we would keep this iteration free of influence and actually let it grow on its own."

Hartford was momentarily caught off guard. "Harkook!" he shouted in surprise. "What…what are you doing here?" I countered, "You should know, Tolzarx. After all, a foolish leader is one who makes a mess and then forgets to clean it up." Tolzarx flushed deep red and unleashed another mental burst that I/Harkook countered. "I didn't know you were a hypocrite, Harkook," Tolzarx said. "After all, I left this organization untouched and pure. Now you possess the part of this world that I left untouched."

Harkook shook his head sadly. "I am only here with my agents to clean up your foolish mess, Tolzarx," he said. "I cannot let you run amok with every iteration I put up for experimentation. I, after all, am a scientist. You, my dear faker, have great potential but no sense of righteousness. Odlil realized that when I told him what had happened. He, after all, will become the greatest of us all."

Tolzarx did not even bother to respond this time. He unleashed bursts of energy with abandon, firing all around and jeopardizing the stability of the headquarters. Harkook did not try to counter the attacks as he slid around them or reflected them right back at Tolzarx. This only seemed to make Tolzarx even more reckless. His bursts of energy became stronger and threatened to overwhelm Meister's emergency system.

Tolzarx threw Harkook off balance in a gliding motion, changed his energy pulse, and unleashed a smashing spell. Harkook just barely managed to block the blow, absorbing the energy. With a jerk, he disintegrated my body as the absorbed energy swirled around Tolzarx, pinning him to the wall. Harkook rematerialized. "Kneel, Tolzarx," he commanded. Tolzarx resisted. "I said," continued Harkook with a dangerous note in his voice, "*kneel!*" Tolzarx still resisted but gave in at the end. "With the power bestowed upon me as protector of the Republic of the Mind, I hereby depose you, Tolzarx, from power for jeopardizing the safety of the republic."

"Never!" Tolzarx screamed and leered at Harkook. With a final smash, Tolzarx teleported out of the building, shattering his bonds and using the energy generated to smash Harkook into a wall, which knocked him unconscious. This action gave me back control of my body. I struggled against my sudden tiredness. My memories of the events began to slip away as I drifted into a mindless state of stasis.

Karl von Liebnitz

As I finished my rallying cry, the commanders rushed ahead with me to check the arsenals and ensure that everything remained untouched and ready for battle. While I walked down the corridor, I suddenly sensed another mental presence inside the headquarters. The signature was vaguely familiar, but the mental energy was much more powerful than anything that Hartford or I could have generated.

I brushed off the mental presence as a ghost of my imagination. It was impossible that my enemies possessed such a storehouse of mental energy concentrated in one being. Not even Pierre was this powerful. As I was brushing this off, however, a second presence suddenly registered in my mental scope. Now I was worried. One mental spike of that enormous scale was perhaps a fluke. Two...well, if there were two spikes, something was going terribly wrong.

I tried to send a probing mental finger into the slightly familiar presence. I was surprised by what met me. I was repulsed by a wave of evil, the like of which I had never felt before. I had thought that I had been cruel and evil after my rapid transformation from a rising star to the cruelest sadist of them all. Now I felt the true breadth and depth of evil. Compared to this presence, I was but a measly fly in terms of evil.

For the first time in many years, I trembled in fear at the thought of what this presence could do to me with that mental ability. It would wreak havoc upon society ten trillion times worse than what I could ever hope to achieve.

My feelings of doubt about my relative position of power in relation to the world in general returned. All of us hide behind a web of lies and personas. We are all too scared to show our true faces to the world, to give ourselves up to be judged. Some...mental being must be exploiting us because of this fatal deficiency. We are being played like pigs led to slaughter.

My heart almost stopped as I heard a sound. The emergency alarm began wailing as a lockdown was set in motion. Quivering with tension, I checked the problem and nearly stopped breathing.

The structural foundations were cracking. Mental spikes were occurring at a rate too fast for me to pick up. Something was happening down in the hangar bay, where Klatschnikov was. Was he another unwitting pawn in this cosmic chess game? Probably so. Why would these mental beings want some half-wits like Klatschnikov as their agents?

A deep boom rumbled through the headquarters, and the entire building shook. Oh God, I thought. This was not good. "Commanders," I shouted into my wristband transmitter, "hold your positions. I repeat, hold your positions. I will keep the situation under control."

I bounded down several flights of stairs at once, not bothering with the elevator. Soon I reached the hangar bay level and rushed toward the area. I was moving so fast with superhuman strength and stamina that I almost ran head-on into the steel bay door. I slowed down enough to punch in the code and disable the security system. Mentally I urged the doors apart with a grating screech. Walking slowly, I was cautious, unsure of what I was going to find. What I did find shocked me. It was carnage.

22

THE BEST DEFENSE IS A STRONG OFFENSE

Pierre Hartford

When I regained consciousness, I opened my eyes and tried to look around. My vision was blurry, but it was enough that I could see the scope of the damage. There was shattered metal everywhere, and I saw a gaping hole in the ceiling. I could feel a few dozen shards of metal embedded in my back. Directly to the left and above me, there was a hole of my shape, beside another human-sized hole through which Mr. Roland must have fallen.

There was no damage other than those two holes, it seemed, from the battle fought between the two mental beings controlling our bodies. Did that mean Mr. Roland's possessor had lifted the vault straight out of space and time even before I had been possessed? If so, Mr. Roland and I had fallen back into reality through a black hole, which no human should be able to survive. We had fallen back through time. But had there even been a battle with time and a black hole? Could this not all be a product of my imagination? Even my memories began to blur as I faded back into unconsciousness.

When I woke up, I was a bit bewildered. Mr. Roland and I were sitting once again at the round table, minus my father. I had been healed, but I had no memory of ever leaving the vault and traveling back up in the elevator. Mr. Roland sat straight across from me, rubbing his eyes and looking just as confused as I was. "You have no memory of the events either, sir?" I asked. Mr. Roland shook his head without saying anything.

"Sir," I said bluntly, "I hate to be this direct, but we need to get to work on mobilization and teleportation to wherever Liebnitz is heading, which should be obvious on our satellite scanner probes. You have to stop lolling around without a purpose and get some life back. We can get your wife and children back but only if we successfully complete the task ahead of us. You need to regain your goals so you can function productively."

"Yes," Mr. Roland replied. Almost immediately, he sat up and showed some vigor, no longer looking like an ancient man. He jumped up and almost flew straight down to the arsenal to pick up the weapons when I erected a barrier to hold him back. "Slow down, sir," I said, wincing as Mr. Roland almost broke the bonds holding him back.

"Why, Pierre?" he asked with sudden concern. "Because we still have to discuss battle plans and find Liebnitz before we travel to the field!" I screamed, surprising myself more than

I surprised Mr. Roland with my sudden outburst. He looked thunderstruck because I had gone over the edge and lost my temper over some minor issues.

"Uh, Pierre," he said in a conciliatory tone, "calm down, bud. Jeez. If you want to discuss plans and locate Liebnitz first, we can do that." As quickly as my anger arose, it evaporated. There was definitely something weird about this whole Liebnitz business. "OK," I said with sudden calmness.

"This entire battle is going to devolve into hand-to-hand combat, while mental abilities will attempt to tilt the field one way or the other. Based on that premise, we should keep soldiers in reserve to drop in on mobile command posts, which other soldiers will congregate to as a last stand against Liebnitz's forces. The last-stand incentive will give us an advantage in morale and help combat the inevitable fact that most of our forces will be dead if we win. It's a simple plan that will be devastatingly effective."

Mr. Roland nodded in agreement. "Most definitely so, Pierre. Simple but devastatingly effective at the same time. Now, as for Liebnitz and where he is congregating." He moved toward the command station at the end of the hall, but I motioned for him to stop and watch. I mimed grabbing onto a circular object and slowly moved my hand sideways. A laser map appeared out of thin air. It hovered in midair, above the table, and I activated it.

Mr. Roland's mouth fell open. "You have a strong mind, Pierre," he finally said. "Imagination is a gift that not many people possess, especially not those with mental abilities." The map beeped, and Mr. Roland turned to look at it. The three-dimensional map glittered with dots of light representing many different things, but two dots stood out above the rest. "That blue dot is Liebnitz's headquarters," said Mr. Roland, "and the green dot is where the mobilization is taking place. He's being smart. We're going to be fighting in an unfamiliar urban environment. The city of Bonn, Germany, it says on the map."

"But that plays right into our hands!" I said ecstatically. "All the better to set up command posts and mow down Liebnitz's troops! A city environment will be equally brutal for both sides!" Mr. Roland had another idea though. "Can't you just imagine setting up an army with your powers?" he asked. I shook my head. "The power requirement would be many times what I can accumulate and unleash," I replied. "I can only imagine things for you and me, as well as things that can neutralize Dad and Liebnitz."

"Very well," said Mr. Roland. "The arsenal is good to go. We just need to distribute the weaponry and brief the troops. Then we shall teleport to Bonn and begin the battle that will determine the fate of the earth."

Later I wondered why I hadn't noticed that something was wrong with both our thoughts and our emotions.

Karl von Liebnitz

Klatschnikov had been brutally stuffed into a hole in the wall that was exactly his size. The pillars were crumbling and rubble lay everywhere. Dust permeated the air. Remnants of the mental presence that I had felt in the air were spread throughout the room. The air was bending as wormholes snapped open and shut with disturbing regularity.

Klatschnikov groaned and stirred from his elevated position. With a crack, the wall crumbled to pieces and Klatschnikov fell out. "What happened, Yuri?" I asked. He responded urgently and forcefully, but I did not understand a word of the Russian he spoke. "Yuri," I said, cutting off his tirade, "speak German." Klatschnikov nodded as if he understood and began to speak German. "Crumbles…God faker…warp," he mumbled. The effort proved to be too much for him, and he fell unconscious again.

I lifted him off the floor and brought him with me to the stairs. He was injured quite extensively, it seemed. Being stuffed into the wall had probably broken half the bones in his body and ruined his armor. Besides that, his brain must have been fried to almost nothingness, with the mental spikes going on and whatever else had happened.

It seemed there had been "beings" that had come to him as God and been exposed as fakers, leading to a possession of his body and a battle. As soon as I had come up with this concept, a presence that was foreign to me seemed to pervade my mind. I slumped unconscious on the stairs, feeling my memories fade away.

I woke up in my office and realized that I had been tampered with. So had Klatschnikov and the other commanders. The building had been fixed so it seemed as if nothing had happened, that we were just mobilizing for the battle and there had been no emergency. I knew there was tampering, but I could not remember anything, so I was at a loss as to what I should do.

I assumed that we would continue with the Bonn plan. I switched on the intercom system. "Commanders," I said calmly. I received replies that indicated they were receiving the message.

"Are the mobilizations ready for battle?" I asked. All of the replies were in the affirmative. "I am in charge of the coup de grace. You know your units and positions in the Bonn plan. You know our strategy. With this, we will win, and the age of Tyrannei will begin. To Bonn we go!" I finished. "To Bonn we go!" my commanders shouted through the intercom.

Bonn, Tyrannei Sector 13-23

As both sides in the battle of the world hurried toward Bonn, Will Hartford had different plans. He knew that they were fighting there, but he had no interest in heading to Bonn to join the scrum. He must show them everything in one stroke. They would all be together and worn out, and nothing would stand in the way of his domination of this reality. He would be a god, and what a god he would be.

Pierre and Mr. Roland teleported to the west side of Bonn, taking along the entire shock trooper forces and setting up their command post outside of the city. "Sir," said Pierre, "I will join the battle, and you should stay here to deliver the orders for all to hear and follow." Mr. Roland nodded. "Good idea, Pierre," he said. Weapons were distributed to all of the shock troopers. They each received a set of low-purity clerium armor, two laser pistols, an anti-vehicle missile launcher, and various weapon parts to make an acid-bullet turret or a flaming sniper rifle. Parts for the mobile command posts would be dropped by the jets, which were equipped with missiles to blast the city to shreds. There were also tanks and heavy artillery in reserve at the command post manned by Mr. Roland.

Tyrannei and Liebnitz teleported out of headquarters and emerged in the center of Bonn. Liebnitz's troops were issued low-purity shuritanium armor, which contained a reflective force field, as well as electrostatic dispersers, pulsars, laser-equipped missile launchers, and acidic bullet sprayers. Kept in reserve were many secret inventions that were controlled by a computer system Liebnitz manned from his elevated command post. His commanders would be posted on the ground, helping facilitate the ruse of a frontal assault to draw Pierre and Mr. Roland into Klatschnikov's trap on the flanks.

As the armies prepared to fight, Liebnitz picked up signals on his radar. "Commanders," he said into his radio, "enemies moving into the city. Charge and prepare to engage." Tyrannei's advance troops moved out with the commanders, fanning out in every direction and bravely charging through the suburbs. Mr. Roland spoke into his radio as well. "Pierre, Liebnitz has noticed our movements. Hostiles moving out of the city center toward our positions. Last-stand posts being parachuted into areas where troops are in need of them."

"Yes sir," replied Pierre. The troops formed into circles as last-stand posts were parachuted down. The posts were quickly filled, weapons were assembled, and soldiers were dispersed in all directions. The three divisions that were to charge from the sides hoped for the best and set out to do their duty. Pierre prepared to move from one post to another to help out and thin the ranks of the enemy so he could end the battle once and for all.

Mr. Roland also decided to begin shelling the city center

and surrounding areas. With resounding blasts, the entire line of artillery went off, tank shells were lobbed onto the advancing troops, and laser missiles were released by the jets. After a few hits by heavy artillery, Liebnitz quickly erected his force field and the shells smashed into the field, making the whole shield shudder from the impact. Just as quickly, the low-purity shuritanium armor of the soldiers was unsheathed, and the tank shells only served to smash the buildings.

Despite the continuing bombardment from the autoloading weapons, the Tyrannei troops finally reached the line of last-stand posts. With a rolling crackle, the soldiers began to fire into the horde of Tyrannei troops, not doing any damage with the first wave of bullets. However, Pierre had wisely installed autoteleporters on the bullets that flew through the armor and began mowing down the troops, not merely stunning them. At the same time, Pierre's advance forces were surrounded on three sides while the rest of the shock troopers charged the city center.

The battle dragged on, and the Tyrannei troops began to seek cover in buildings, for they realized they would not advance through their brute-force tactics. Even then, however, the troops still died rapidly as lethal snipers among the shock troopers quickly killed off the exposed soldiers with lasers, acid, and flames. The remainder of the once great Tyrannei first wave cowered in the buildings, not daring to move for fear of being shot down.

With a mental wrench, Pierre leveled the entire block of buildings in front of where the troops had been hiding. The buildings came crashing down, killing the remainder of the enemy's first wave. The first wave of Tyrannei had been defeated, with few casualties for Pierre and Mr. Roland as a result. Overall, it was a success for both of them. "Pierre, don't let your guard down yet," Mr. Roland said through his radio, cutting short the victory celebrations. "Liebnitz is sending out his secret weapon. You might want to start getting worried."

23

THE IMPOSSIBLE BECOMES POSSIBLE

Bonn, Tyrannei Sector 13-23

As Liebnitz had expected, most of the commanders, except for Klatschnikov, Bartleby, and Joubert, had been killed in the first wave. Liebnitz felt no need to spare the lives of his recruits painstakingly gathered over the decades.

With this new army of his, he would no longer have any need for many humans, just a few select commanders. The recruits had valiantly done their job. They had softened up Pierre and Mr. Roland, making the job that much easier for his second wave.

The second wave combined the pinnacles of his inventions. It was an army of robots, controlled by a robotic consciousness. But these robots were not just any ordinary robots. Their consciousness was the first true artificial intelligence. It passed the Turing test with ease and could outwit most living humans. However, it could not outwit Liebnitz, which was a good thing.

How had Liebnitz even come up with this level of AI? He had solved that vexing conundrum called quantum computing. After limited success at computing levels beyond five hundred atoms, Liebnitz had reinvented the basic architecture of quantum computing and arranged the atoms into the shape of a parallel processor rather than an endless row. The parallel processor was repeated over and over until the number of atoms computing data reached trillions.

Computer calculations were so effortless and fast and the success was so widespread that Liebnitz made the computer the administrator of the organization, under his direct control. The computer was also remodeled into a neural network, where it quickly reached AI status.

Controlled by this beast of a computing machine, the robots were smarter than the entire forces that Pierre and Mr. Roland controlled. Only Pierre could perhaps stop these robots, and even he could not defeat millions upon millions of them at once, especially with the new advanced weapon modules built onto their exoskeletons. The system was virtually impenetrable, and Pierre could never hack the mainframe in time to shut down the core of the system and turn his sights on Liebnitz.

When Pierre heard Mr. Roland's comments, he mentally gulped. He was assuming robots, obviously, after such a failure by vulnerable humans who might have been just cannon fodder. The robots would be virtually invulnerable. What mattered was the level of intelligence and how that intelligence had been reached.

As the robots came into sight, Pierre realized that their level of intelligence was far above human intelligence levels. Most definitely true AI was at play here. Pierre mentally probed the mainframe controlling the robots. Quantum computing! True quantum computers were a legend, a myth. For Liebnitz to have one…no wonder his system was unhackable, except for a few weak spots.

Pierre nearly lost faith in his abilities at the mental sight of a functioning quantum computer that was running calculations using a few trillion atoms, but he decided he must soldier on. "Men," he called out through his radio to the last-stand posts, "hold your fire until I give the command." Cries of assent came back through the radio. The robots continued to sprint toward the men, who were unsheathing their weapons and armor. "Surrender or die!" they screeched continuously. The men trembled but held their positions, weapons trained.

"You shall die!" screeched the robots, but the men didn't back down. With an outburst of energy, the robots' weapons began to fire, killing a few men here and there with a few lucky shots that penetrated their clerium armor. With a sudden leap, the robots jumped high into the air and disappeared. The men blinked and wondered what had just happened. So did Pierre and Mr. Roland.

Suddenly Pierre knew, and it was as if his soul had just fallen through the ground. "Men!" he screamed. "Get your damn weapons pointing up now!" The men scrambled to comply with Pierre's unexpected burst of panic. "Mr. Roland," Pierre stammered through the connection, "get all weapons firing up at the sky. Everything. Now. I know what I'm doing." All parties scrambled to comply with Pierre's seemingly confusing order.

All was for naught, however, as it was too little, too late. The robots crashed back down to the earth, smashing through the last-stand posts and onto the men. All weapons were firing into the sky, but they were hitting too few robots to combat the millions that swarmed onto the posts. The men fought back valiantly, but soon most of them were dead, mowed down by the robots.

A few had survived and were fighting back, smartly destroying some robots and dodging others. They were holding their own but wearing out, and soon they, too, would die like their brave comrades. Liebnitz smiled as his plan had worked perfectly. "Klatschnikov, Bartleby, Joubert," he said into his radio, "get ready to receive the rest of the troops. I think they'll be coming your way soon."

Pierre realized that fighting back was hopeless, and he decided to try to flank Liebnitz. "Men," he shouted into his radio, "retreat and return to me. We're going to try to flank Liebnitz. Half of you go to Liebnitz's right flank, the rest of you with me." The cries of assent came back through the radio, and Pierre regrouped with half of the survivors to Liebnitz's left flank.

He felt a pit of dread in his stomach as he saw how few of the men remained but decided that he would not lose hope. He would try his best to break the flank of Liebnitz's forces. As he and his forces rounded the corner of one of the buildings on the edge of Bonn, Pierre saw what he was going up against. Half of Liebnitz's tanks and the majority of his air force were amassed against Pierre and his meager forces.

Ten million robots stood in line, ready to fire upon his forces and kill them. Klatschnikov and Joubert stood with grins on their faces, Klatschnikov resting his hand on a big red button. Pierre knew that probably meant Bartleby controlled the rest of Liebnitz's forces and another ten million robots. With a feeling of tremendous guilt, Pierre ordered the remainder of his forces to attack.

With one leap, the robots surrounded the men. Surprisingly, they did not immediately fire upon them. Klatschnikov looked at the men, then looked directly at Pierre, and burst into laughter. When he could finally speak, he said, "Here we see Pierre Hartford, humiliated and about to be defeated. The robots are about to eradicate his meager forces that could have defeated Tyrannei once and for all.

"But wait!" said Klatschnikov, making Pierre look up in surprise. "What if the robots were to have, say, a bug in their code that would incapacitate all of them? What if the forces they were about to destroy still had a chance?" As he finished his sentence, the robots screamed and began to violently shake and then collapsed to the ground. Pierre's men shouted with joy and began to recklessly charge Klatschnikov and Joubert.

"But wait...," Klatschnikov's voice cut through the cheers of the men. "What could this big red button that I'm so casually leaning on be? Should we find out?" Without waiting for a reply, Klatschnikov threw himself on the button. Pierre saw what was happening and quickly teleported to a point far behind his men.

For a second, it seemed as if Klatschnikov's button didn't work. The men continued to run forward. Then, with a boom that shook the earth and toppled some of the buildings in Bonn, the tanks and jets fired their weapons and exploded. Pierre's men were directly in the line of fire. In the blinding light, Pierre could only see a giant cloud of ash and some random body parts flying through the air, but he heard the shouts of his men turn into screams. Klatschnikov laughed out loud, for he knew that Pierre's forces were defeated and that Tyrannei had won.

Pierre screamed in frustration and broke off all connections to Mr. Roland. Mr. Roland knew what had happened and shivered in horror at the rage he knew Pierre was about to unleash upon the entire city of Bonn. Pierre broke all moral bonds of self-control, unleashed the rage he had held in check for so long inside of him, and let it loose. His mental energy increased twentyfold, and he concentrated his smashing blows on Liebnitz's quantum computer. The mainframe shook as it tried to withstand the crippling blows, but Pierre did not relent. The computer was at the brink of shutting down, and Liebnitz was beginning to panic.

An explosion of mental energy emanated from Pierre and engulfed Klatschnikov and Joubert. Once the wave of energy reached Joubert, he was instantly vaporized. It was as if he had never existed; he was gone without a trace. A golden shield suddenly appeared around Klatschnikov and protected him from the wave of mental energy. His mouth hung open with shock. Pierre decided to press his advantage.

Will, however, chose this moment to enter the scene. The moment he teleported into Bonn, Tolzarx shattered his mind and destroyed all remnants of Will's soul, erasing him from reality forever and making himself the new Will Hartford. "Hold it, hold it, all of you," said the new Will calmly. Pierre and Liebnitz were in shock when they saw him enter the city. So were the remaining survivors, including Bartleby's forces and Mr. Roland, and all fighting miraculously ceased.

"I am the new Will Hartford," he announced. "The insidious snake that you all once knew as Will Hartford has been erased from reality. The old Will Hartford is gone forever, never to come back in this form. I was once known as Tolzarx among my compatriots, but I will be known as Will Hartford in this reality. Odlil, Harkook, Xaleg, Alarkabac, and Zarjo, make yourselves known. We all know that the time for letting this reality run amok in my mind is over. Odlil, Harkook, and Xaleg, you have fought brilliantly but have been outclassed."

Pierre burst out with "I am Odlil!" Then Klatschnikov came forward as Harkook, Liebnitz as Xaleg, Mr. Roland as Alarkabac, and Bartleby as Zarjo. "None of you will take control, for what I want to see is these creations' reactions to the truth. I want to see the shock on their faces as I kill their reality and show them what all of this really is," said the new Will.

"You see," he continued, "this world is not really what you puny idiots think it is. This world is not real. You here, all of you, are products of my mind. You are on a level of my subconscious. Your entire universe is contained within one level of my dreams. All of you are products of my dream world.

"In the real world, I am the leader of a society of beings made up of pure mental energy. We stand for experimentation in the subconscious mind. My mind was used as an experimental breeding ground, with Harkook as the supervisor. This means that Harkook designed the experiments, and I created them. However, differences arose between us, leading to a grand debate on the real meaning of science.

"Nominally Harkook won the debate, but in truth, I did not concede defeat. This experiment was created to see what would happen to a dream if it were left unchecked and unsupervised, allowing the subconscious mind to advance the plot of the reality, to put it simply. Your world, however, was the one that produced the most worrying results. When we let you imbeciles run amok, you created this fiasco between good and evil, one of the most ancient and deep-rooted archetypes of the mind.

"In this case, however, both sides were flawed, and you were going to kill yourselves off. Out of the goodness of my heart, I decided to step in and become a benevolent dictator. I can do this by possessing your minds and controlling you, no matter what actions you take. This leads to you having mental abilities of some degree or other, depending on how much energy you put into possessing your target and the amount of power that you have.

"Harkook was enraged that I, along with my cronies, broke the principle of noninterference, so he and his camp decided to intervene when things came to a head. In that way, I maneuvered you into this position, and now Harkook knows it is too late for him to stop me from destroying his 'promising experiment.' For now we know the true consequences of leaving the subconscious unchecked, and we will never commit this fatal error again."

Pierre and Liebnitz suddenly understood the strange circumstances that had been plaguing them throughout the entire buildup, and they were extremely shocked, as were Mr. Roland and Klatschnikov. Just as the shock subsided, rage boiled up in Pierre's and Liebnitz's hearts. They had been played like fools. Puppet strings had jerked them into this position after their free will had evaporated. They wanted revenge, and they wanted it now.

However, just as they were going to get their revenge by unleashing devastation on the world using mental energy, the beings took possession of them. Odlil, Harkook, and Xaleg channeled the rage and did the right thing: they fired a concentrated beam of energy at Tolzarx. Zarjo and Alarkabac watched helplessly, too slow to react, as Tolzarx was struck down.

"Shatter the dream!" shouted Odlil, Harkook, and Xaleg. Tolzarx realized what was happening too late. The three burst into waves of mental energy, the power of which was off the charts in intensity. The world began to disintegrate around Bonn, and Tolzarx began to scream as his new body began to painfully dissolve. As Tolzarx disintegrated, he exploded, and it was too much for the reality in his subconscious.

The dream exploded and shattered, and everything went into complete darkness. A vortex opened, sucking into it the remnants of Pierre, Klatschnikov, and Liebnitz. The other three possessed disappeared into a separate black hole. They did not know where they were going, and for now, they were trapped in space and time. As the vortex swirled, the first three dissolved into the whirlpool of energy and swung around out of the dream. With a final burst of energy, the dream disappeared and the vortex emptied into a blank white room. Pierre, Klatschnikov, and Liebnitz tumbled out and smashed straight into the walls of the room, losing consciousness instantly.

Elsewhere, an entity felt the smash into reality from Tolzarx's subconscious and was shocked to the very core. The impossible had been achieved. The experimentation had created a shattered dream. Dreamland had blurred with reality, and the dream had come into reality. Humans, as they called themselves, had become real. The mental beings had achieved one of the greatest feats of all eternity. They had produced children.

To be continued in: Children of the Gods

GERMAN GLOSSARY

Aus dem Weg! – Out of the way!

Da ist ein Anruf von Klatschnikov – Klatschnikov is calling

Da ist keine Spur – There is no trace

das Vaterland – the fatherland

der alte – the old

der Tag – the day

Du hast gerufen? – Did you call?

Er ist noch ein kleines Kind! – He is still a little child!

Freund(e) – friend(s)

Genug! – Enough!

Gut – good

hier spricht Yuri – this is Yuri

ich bin kein Dummkopf – I'm not a fool

ja – yes

jung nochmal – young again

Komm schnell! – Come quickly!

Mach es nicht, Mutti! – Don't do it, Mom!

Meister – master, boss

mit den Puppen – with the puppets

nein – no

Stopp! – Stop!

Tschüs – bye-bye
Tyrannei – tyranny
Warte – wait
Was? – What?
weg – gone

ACKNOWLEDGMENTS

I would like to thank Mr. Tim Campbell, my former humanities teacher, for reading my first draft and giving me many suggestions and a lot of support. I would also like to thank the staff at Outskirts Press, Inc., for editing the manuscript and helping with the cover design and distribution of the book.

CPSIA information can be obtained
at www.ICGtesting.com
Printed in the USA
BVHW070737110720
583415BV00003B/235